Look for my new Center Tales on Amazon Books.

Comments? drhuf123@gmail.com

The Prophet Ezekiel

by

Dave Huffstetler

Dave Huffstetler

This book is available at Quail Ridge Books.

The contents of this work, including, but not limited to, the accuracy of events, people, and places depicted; opinions expressed; permission to use previously published materials included; and any advice given or actions advocated are solely the responsibility of the author, who assumes all liability for said work and indemnifies the publisher against any claims stemming from publication of the work.

All Rights Reserved
Copyright © 2024 by Dave Huffstetler

No part of this book may be reproduced or transmitted, downloaded, distributed, reverse engineered, or stored in or introduced into any information storage and retrieval system, in any form or by any means, including photocopying, and recording, whether electronic or mechanical, now known or hereinafter invented without permission in writing from the publisher.

RoseDog Books
585 Alpha Drive, Suite 103
Pittsburgh, PA 15238
Visit our website at *www.rosedogbookstore.com*

ISBN: 979-8-89211-308-3
eISBN: 979-8-89211-806-4

SISTER ALMA

PART I

Elmer looked at himself in the cracked full-length mirror screwed into the front of the bathroom door. He had just pulled on his newest Osh Kosh overalls and had hiked the galluses up over his best white shirt.

Elmer turned sideways and kinda sucked in his belly; "Bet she'll like this," he thought. He pulled on his Sunday shoes and got his best hat out of the closet, then went out of the bedroom and walked down the hall to the living room, where Bert, his wife, and little ten year old Nan were waiting.

Bert said "You look nice, Elmer, but we need to go if we're going to make it to the camp meeting on time. You need to load up those two hams also." Elmer grunted and went out to the smokehouse and plucked two salt cured hams from the ceiling joists where they were suspended on nails with twine. He looked at the remaining two hams and thought of those Poland-China Hogs they had slaughtered last winter. "Good ones," he thought to himself, and carried the meat and put it in the trunk of the car.

By this time Bert and Nan had come out of the house and got in the car, Nan in the back seat. Elmer drove around the little circular drive in front of the house and rolled down the hill toward the country road. His house sat up on a pretty knoll, and the land dropped away from it all around, pastures in the front and woods in the back.

"How much you gonna charge Granny Elmer?" Bert asked, surveying Nan in the back seat and wondering if her fingernails were dirty.

"I reckon 'bout twelve dollars, she is my momma ya know."

"Guess that's fair enough," Bert offered, "since hog meat is a little scarce this year."

"Sister Alma is gonna take us to 'Joy and Praise Camp' this summer if we are all real good," Nan said. Cousin Helene said Aunt Pearl was gonna let her go too! It's gonna be up toward the mountains, near Lake Lure, and we can go swimmin' and everything."

"Oh, I'm sure you'll be goin' Nan. There's more coming to Sister Alma's camp meetin' all the time, so I 'spect there will be a lot of kids to take, and you know it would be a wonderful, loving Christian atmosphere if Sister Alma is running it," Bert exclaimed, and told Elmer to quit driving so slow.

"You drive like an old man," she said. Elmer made no comment and continued to negotiate the old Ford around the curves to Russ and Sarah's. Russ was Elmer's baby brother, and Sarah was his redheaded Scotch Irish wife. They lived with Granny, Elmer and Russ' mother, in the "old house," the homeplace where the Hoffman clan had been raised. It was an old two-story clapboard house that had never been painted, and had a 5 V tin roof, a well, and an outhouse. There was also a root cellar. Russ and Sarah had one girl, Lois. Lois was Nan's age.

The old house sat down in a hollow and Elmer slowly negotiated the sharp turn off the country road, up next to the Wild Cherry tree that was so bad to get bag worms. It was six o'clock on a warm July afternoon, and they were all starting to sweat a little bit as they piled out of the car. Elmer, Bert and Nan walked down the little well-worn path to the L shaped porch at the right rear of the house. The open area at the L was where the chickens congregated, so it was totally devoid of grass – you really had to watch your step when you were heading to the porch.

Lois was up in the big Chinaberry tree that covered the chicken yard. She hollered hello and climbed down the tree hanging onto the little pieces of wood her daddy had nailed into the tree, like ladder rungs.

"Hey, Lois, you going to Camp Joy and Praise?" Nan shouted exuberantly.

"I don't know for sure, Nan," Lois said, and changed the subject quickly. "Want a biscuit and molasses? Momma just pulled out some hot biscuits and we got some of Mr. Beam's molasses, the best around."

"Sure," said Nan, and they trooped up onto the porch and into the kitchen where a slender red-haired woman with bright green eyes was placing biscuits on a platter.

"Hey Nan," said Sarah, and having overheard Lois asked, "How about a hot biscuit with butter and molasses; just churned the butter yesterday."

Nan's eyes got big; like most of the Hoffmans she did not lack for appetite. "Yes ma'am," Nan cried, and Sarah fixed her up a little plate of butter and molasses and cut open a steaming hot biscuit and laid it beside the sweet stuff.

Elmer opened the screened door for Bert and they entered the kitchen at the same time that Russ walked in from the little room beside the kitchen, which went down a step. It was kind of a small family room, and had a little fireplace in it – a cozy nook.

"How ya'll doing," said Russ, grinning his big grin with the perfect teeth. He was in an old pair of overalls and nothing else, having come in from work at Seth Lumber Co., and changed into comfortable duds.

Then Granny, Russ and Elmer's mother, came in the kitchen from the porch. She had been out scratching in her flowers.

"Hello Elmer, Bert, and look there at little Nan; whatcha doin' little girl?" Nan grinned at her granny, brown molasses dripping down the right side of her chin.

Granny was the prototype granny of the 1940's in the country; bent over, toothless, hair skinned back in a tight bun. A pair of very thick silver rimmed spectacles sat on her nose, a testimony to her cataract removal.

"Let's sit out on the porch," Granny suggested, and they all left the kitchen, Nan finishing her treat quickly, and found seats on the wooden floored porch. It had cooled down a little in the late afternoon, and the porch faced east.

"Well what are you all doin' all dressed up in the middle of the week," asked Russ, giving Sarah a very quick little wink.

"We are goin' down to the camp meetin' at Dallas to hear Sister Alma; they say she is going to have a healing service tonight, and I would not want to miss that. Ya know she had one last week and Bogus got up there on the stage - you know he has always been plagued with terrible migraine headaches – and she prayed over him and he said he ain't had one since," Bert exclaimed.

Russ chuckled and said, "Maybe he should have got her to restore those four fingers he got caught in the planing machine last March."

Sarah smiled, but Granny said, "Now Russ, I have heard of such things, and I ain't sure it is right Godly to poke fun at it."

"Okay, Mom," Russ said.

"Elmer, did you bring that ham you were talking about; you know we're out of meat," Granny asked.

"Yep, Momma, let me get it out of the trunk," he said and went to the old Ford, returning with the ham, one of the two he had plucked from the smoke house. Elmer laid it down on the floor of the porch and Granny said, "Lois, get me a butcher knife so's I can cut a little piece of this to suck on; it looks like a real good one."

Lois brought the knife and Granny sliced a little chip off the side and popped it in her mouth. "Mm-mm," Granny said, as she sucked on the salty meat. "That is mighty good ham Elmer, can I offer to pay you?" Granny asked.

"I guess twelve dollars will do it," Elmer said, and kind of looked over toward the chinaberry tree.

Granny paused a moment, then said, "Lois, get my pocket book out of the wardrobe."

Lois came back directly with Granny's pocketbook, and Granny counted out two fives and two ones.

Russ and Sarah exchanged very quick embarrassed glances as Elmer rolled up the money and dropped it in the top pocket of his overalls.

Bert said, "I reckon we oughta get on now; ya'll come and see us when you can."

Russ smiled and said, "Okay Bert, we'll see you soon."

Elmer looked at Russ a little sheepishly and said, "Bye Russ," then stooped down to hug his momma. Sarah smiled and said nothing.

"Now Cousin Lois, you be sure and beg your momma and daddy to come to Sister Alma's Joy and Praise Camp, cause we're gonna sing songs and swim and everything," shouted Nan as she trundled off behind her parents to the car.

They got in the old Ford and started up the dusty road out to Highway 321, two miles of red dirt, and then three more to go on the blacktop before they got to Dallas.

Nobody said anything for a while; they just sat on the porch as the afternoon cooled off.

Granny finally said, "Russ, will you hang that ham up down in the smoke house, but cut off a slab first, and we'll have it at breakfast."

"Sure, Mom," said Russ and hoisted the meat up and walked barefoot the thirty feet to the empty smoke house.

The four of them ate supper quietly, with only a scattering of comments, mostly from Lois. She was a good science student and was excited about going into the sixth grade, the first opportunity to use a microscope.

"You know, there are germs everywhere," Lois pronounced. "Well I guarantee you they are all over that ham." Russ and Sarah said nothing, just grinned at each other, but Granny spoke up.

"Now youngun, I bet it would take a legion of soldiers to keep you away from that nasty ham tomorrow mornin' when you got eggs, grits, and your momma's biscuits together with it."

They all laughed, and Lois said, "Yes ma'am, you have got me there, so I guess some of them germs must be okay. Anyway, they sure do taste good."

After supper they all went back out onto the porch and walked around to the front of the house and sat in the little stiff-backed chairs on the front porch. The chairs had comfortable leather laced bottoms, and everybody sat in those except Granny, who had a small rocker out there with a cushion on it.

The house faced due west and looking across the road beyond the broom straw field, the sun was setting quickly.

"I think that would be a pretty spot for a house, don't you Sarah?" Russ said, pointing beyond the Wild Cherry tree to the broom straw field. The land sloped gently left to right, with the center area being pretty level.

"Well Russ, if we keep selling butter and eggs up on the mill hill at Harden, and you keep workin', and we save our money, maybe someday we can do that," Sarah said, with a wistful look in her eye.

"That would be the way to do it alright," nodded Granny. The air was cooling and it was quiet for a long time. Lightning bugs started to come out, and Lois ran and caught a couple, putting them in a small jar and screwing on the lid.

"Wonder what's happenin' at the the camp meeting?" Granny said.

Bert was practicing her songs in her mind; she knew at least three of them: <u>Bringing in the Sheaves</u>, <u>Are You Washed in the Blood of the Lamb</u>, and the standard end of the night clincher, <u>Just as I am</u>. Sister Alma said <u>Bringing in the Sheaves</u> would strike a chord with the farm community 'cause harvest time was nearing.

Bert was the organist for the camp meetings, and Elmer served as the head usher; his responsibilities included recruiting other ushers and, at the end of the night, counting the money and making note of the other offerings. Out in the country farm goods and even animals were sometimes brought to the meeting as offerings. In the same vein it was not uncommon to hear about Dr. Fesperman in Lincolnton receiving two laying hens and a hunting dog for delivering one of Adrian Clemmer's daughters.

Elmer maneuvered the old Ford into the parking area adjacent to the big brown tent; it looked like a circus tent, with poles spaced throughout and staked off with ropes for support. Iron stobs driven into the Gaston County red clay secured the ropes.

There was plenty of parking and it was surely needed; by the time things got hopping 'bout 7:30 two hundred cars would surround the tent. But now it was just 6:15, and only a smattering of vehicles were present, mostly other ushers.

"Okay, let's go on in," said Elmer, "Going to be a big night, and Sister Alma is going to finish it up with a special healing service. I hear that club footed sister-in-law of Stan Glenn is coming and Joe Clonger said Uncle Joe Clemmer might try to make it, if the arthritis ain't got him so bad."

"Uncle Joe" Clemmer was not a relative, but everybody called him Uncle Joe. He was so afflicted with severe arthritis that he was bent over at a thirty degree angle and got around with two walking sticks.

The trio got out of the car, Elmer retrieving the ham from the trunk. Nan ran off to play with other "Joy and Praise" recruits, and Bert went over to the side of the stage where the old organ was. It had been donated by Mayor Maxwell, a most devoted attendee.

Elmer carried the ham inside the tent, and noticing that no one else was around, walked around behind the stage to where a little 8' x 8' area was cordoned off with curtains. This was Sister Alma's dressing room, where she would change into the tight sparkly evening gowns she was renowned for.

Elmer stepped outside the little partition and called "Sister Alma." In a moment the curtain was pulled back by a tall raven-haired woman with bright red nail polish on her fingernails.

"Come in, Elmer, I just got into my dress. If you had been a few minutes earlier you could have hooked it in the back." Sister Alma was resplendent in a long gown made of a shiny red material with sequins. Although the dress went nearly to her ankles, there was a slit up the left side that went six inches above her knee.

Sister Alma deftly reached behind her neck and quickly unhooked the fastener, pulling the zipper down a few inches.

"Why Elmer, I don't believe I did get that fastened securely in the back after all; can you take a look at it and fix it?"

Elmer was standing there four feet away from her, trance like, and when she said this he dropped the ham to the sawdust floor and moved toward her. Sister Alma turned around so Elmer could reach the zipper and clasp; he clumsily worked the zipper, exploring with his eyes as far down her back as he could. The clasp took a while, big nervous fingers working with a tiny hook and eye.

Once she felt the clasp engage, Sister Alma turned around to face Elmer quickly, startling him as he saw her low cut dress and magnificent bosom looming only inches away.

"What do you have for me tonight, Elmer?" she asked quietly, putting her hand on his shoulder, then placing her arm around his.

"H-h-ham, I brung you a ham," Elmer stammered.

"Oh, my," she exclaimed, "Are you sure? I know meat is hard to come by this year."

"Not a problem," Elmer said, "I've got a-plenty."

Elmer hoisted the ham up onto the small table in the enclosure, mumbling something about ushers and pushed his way through the curtain.

Alma chuckled to herself, looking at the fine ham on the table. "Looks as good as the one his brother Theodore brought last week" she thought, and started painting her full lips bright red. "Great with my dazzling blue eyes," she thought, as she put on the finishing touches looking in the mirror hung from the curtain rod.

Elmer walked out in front of the stage, then stopped to try to collect himself. "I saw halfway down her back," he thought, as he tried to control his breathing. He fumbled in his pocket for a blood pressure pill; he was sure it must be off the chart.

Elmer stood there a few minutes and surveyed the stream of people entering the tent. He saw a lot of familiar faces, but directed his blue eyes, (Sister Alma had mentioned them last week), to the first two rows to the right of the stage. That's where he had instructed the usher candidates to assemble.

Ushering at Sister Alma's event was an honor, and not something to be taken lightly. Elmer puffed up a little bit with the realization that the lovely Sister Alma had entrusted him with this task, and additionally had awarded him the honor of counting the money and accounting for the offerings at the end of the night.

"Quite a responsibility," he thought to himself soberly, and looked at the usher spot. He immediately noticed Joe Beck Clonger, Bogus Clonger, Preacher Clonger; good God he thought, a bumper Clonger night. They would all do, cause they cleaned up good. He looked on down the line and there was Ralph Fulbright – they called him half bright – and Elmer figgered he would be okay. Ushers didn't need to talk, only accept offerings.

"Yea," he thought, "That bunch will be alright." Then he saw Hoover Carpenter and Pasour Rhyne. "My God," he uttered under his breath. Hoover hadn't shaved in 3 days and Elmer knew by his stench he hadn't bathed in a week. He walked over to Hoover.

"Hoover, I told you they wouldn't be no way you could usher if you didn't look respectable and cleaned up."

Hoover briefly looked at Elmer, then cast his eyes down. Hoover had a lot of trouble looking people in the eye.

"I'm sorry Elmer, Bill Costner has been workin' the shit out of me at the still over at Oodley Creek, and I just didn't have time to get cleaned up. But I brought you a quart."

Hoover managed to make eye contact with Elmer, and he could see this statement had got his attention.

Elmer thought a little, then remembered that Sister Alma had always said that we should help the poor and misguided.

"Okay Hoover, but try to do a little better next time." Elmer leaned down and picked up a bunch of collection plates, handed one to the approved Hoover, and then passed them out to the ones he had already passed favorable judgment on.

"You can just put it in the back seat of my car," he told Hoover, and moved on to Pasour Rhyne.

Pasour Rhyne was sitting there, staring off into space, and moving his arms around; first he would put his forearm up against his forehead and cross his other arm across his midsection. Then he would giggle and flash that vacant grin of his. Elmer had seen it before, as everyone else in the Costner Community had. Pasour had a couple of distinctions goin' for him. The first one was he was a charter member of the Larson-Savoney Society, a secret group that met periodically on the banks of the South Fork River. If you asked him about what they did he would clam up and grin his stupid grin. His second claim, and most important, was he was a certified nut. Papers and all, Pasour had made many trips to the psychiatric ward at Morganton to get his temples shaved and the subsequent electric shock. He would act more normal for a few months, but then he would fall back into doing the weird signs and talking about the Secret Society; then he would shut up when you asked him about it.

His most recent trip to Morganton had been prompted by his burning down Earl Lineberger's barn. He got to go in a squad car that time.

Fortunately Earl was kin, and a good guy, so he did not press charges. Understandably Pasour had never married and lived with his mother.

Elmer looked at Pasour and decided it was too close to another shock treatment to trust him with money. He already had enough ushers anyway. Pasour looked at Elmer, figgering he was not chosen, and slunk off down the aisle to sit with his mother.

The tent was filling rapidly, and Elmer went back over to where Bert was at the organ. As he walked up to her he couldn't help but notice how her calves came down to her feet, with no slimming at all at the ankles. Bert shared this affliction with her sister Pearl, Theodore's wife. The young girls called it "cankles," a combination of calves and ankles. Elmer shivered a bit when he looked at those legs, and immediately his mind raced to a vision of Sister Alma's slender curvaceous legs. The sound of the organ broke Elmer's sensual spell, as Bert started in on "Shall We Gather at the River" on the organ.

That music was the signal that Sister Alma was 'bout ready to start, and as Elmer surveyed the audience he saw that it was close to capacity.

The schedule was that Bert would play through the song once and then pause, with just a few background notes on the old organ, as Sister Alma came out onto the stage.

On perfect cue, Sister Alma appeared; she walked to the edge of the stage, which was four steps up from the seating area, and stood stock still.

Bert was instructed to completely stop playing at the very moment that Alma stopped, staring at the gathering. With no emotion on her face, but displaying her curvaceous body in all her adornment, and pursing her brilliantly red lips, she moved her head slowly 90 degrees to the left, and slowly rotated her beautiful head to the right. The crowd had come to a hushed silence when she had walked out, and watched silently with rapt attention as she completed her 180 degree turn.

Then her head moved back to the front, and she shouted, "Are you ready to praise the Lord?" The parishioners erupted as one, "Yes, Sister Alma," in a thundering roar, then went quiet.

Sister Alma repeated her 180 degree survey, then fronted them again, and looking upward said in a loud voice, "Are you ready to accept sweet sweet Jesus into your evil hearts?"

"Yes, yes, yes," they roared, and the cacophony went on for over a minute, until Sister Alma, beaming from the stage held her shapely arms toward the heavens. Quiet again descended.

"Alright, my children, let us raise our voices to the highest in singing, "Shall We Gather at the River."

Perfectly on cue, Bert roared into the song, singing along as she played. "Shall we gather at the river, the beautiful, the beautiful river, shall we gather at the river, that flows by the throne of God."

The crowd joined in, even Elmer trying to hum along a little. Elmer had paid attention to the lyrics but the whole thing about gathering at a river that flowed by the throne of God did not make a lot of sense to him. "Well, what if God wasn't on his throne when everybody gathered; it would sorta be a waste of time," he thought. Elmer made a mental note to ask Sister Alma about that.

The song was winding down, Sister Alma leading with her sweet soprano voice. As it ended Alma greeted everyone, told them how blessed it was that they were here, and lit into her sermon; it was going to be a short one tonight because it was a healing service. "Shouldn't bore them too much with biblical shit before a healin' service," she had decided, her thought being that she would lose them before the show – and the ensuing collection.

When Bert sounded the last note on the river song Sister Alma stared straight ahead, and said in a low, sultry voice, "Do you love Jesus?" The crowd murmured "Yes, Sister Alma." Then she licked her gorgeous lips and said, in a louder voice, "Do you love Jesus every day of your life?" "Yes, Sister Alma," they responded, increasing the volume as she did. Then she twirled 360 degrees and came back to face them, and Bert hit a resounding note on the organ, so well-rehearsed, and Sister Alma screamed out, "Do you love Jesus with every fiber of your being?" At that the entire group erupted, jumping to their feet, their hands held high and waving, shouting, "Yes, yes, yes" to the mountaintops. Pasour Rhyne stood in the aisle repeating over and over the Larson Savoney sign, and Bogus Clonger jumped up and down waving his diminished digits above his head, tobacco juice dripping down the left side of his chin.

When Sister Alma twirled her bounteous bosom swayed a little up and down, and Elmer, the dutiful and observant servant, made note of this; his mind was overwhelmed with two numbers and a letter – 38D. When he had zipped up Sister Alma's dress, and surreptitiously looked down the back, he had espied her brassiere size.

"My God," he had thought to himself, "she is so big." Bert was a big woman in stature, but she wore a 40A bra, more a testimony to her girth than her breast.

Elmer chastised himself for losing his nerve in the dressing room and vowed to himself to be more assertive in the future. "Reckon I had rather be more insertive, than assertive," he thought to himself, feeling proud of himself for his vocabulary use. Elmer was not educated but he did like words, and phrases. He especially liked the phrase "big ol' gorgeous titties," he thought as he watched the twirl.

Elmer's miscreant musings were interrupted by a commotion at the rear of the tent. A small knot of people was at the back of the aisle, and at the center was a little old man dressed in his best overalls, and a white shirt and a red tie. He wore a new straw hat. Elmer strained to see who it was, but within a few moments it was clear who had entered the arena.

It began as a murmur, but quickly grew into a resounding chant – "Uncle Joe, Uncle Joe, Uncle Joe, Uncle Joe." It was the long awaited arrival of Uncle Joe Clemmer; word had gotten out that he was coming for the cure, but most folks did not believe he would take the plunge into the world of Sister Alma evangelism, for Uncle Joe was a lifelong member of Antioch Lutheran Church in the Costner Community, and they were a right conservative bunch. But after years of suffering, and doctors telling him diagnoses that included "crippling arthritis," and adding the cautionary words "You will just have to learn to live with it," Uncle Joe was ready to give something else a shot, a big ol' religious shot.

Uncle Joe made his way slowly toward the stage; he walked with a cane, or walking stick as most called it, but was also assisted at each side by neighbors, on the right by Cora Reid, an elementary school teacher at Costner, and on the other side by Mary Clonger, wife of Joe Clonger, one of the ushers chosen by Chief Usher Elmer.

The chanting got louder the closer the entourage got to the stage; Sister Alma surveyed the crowd once again: "Boy are they ripe or what," she mused, licking her pouty lips with a darting pink tongue. Her gaze came back to rest on Uncle Joe Clemmer. As he and his helpers approached the stage Elmer and Joe Beck Clonger came forward to assist, for he would have to be carried up the four steps to the stage. As the two men hoisted Uncle Joe up, two others emerged from the crowd to help; a drunken Hoover Carpenter came stumbling forward and fell on top of Cora Reid, who yelped like she had been stung by a hornet. On the other side Pasour Rhyne ran up, grinning maniacally, and flashing the Larson-Savoney sign repeatedly. Elmer saw him coming; he knew how to handle Pasour. Elmer leaned over, and whispered three very important words into Pasour Rhyne's ear – "Morganton, electro shock". Pasour turned stark white, and giving the Larson-Savoney sign one last time, tore off down the aisle like a scalded dog.

Alma adjusted the cleavage on the 38Ds as Elmer and Joe Beck got Uncle Joe Clemmer onto the flat surface of the stage. Sister Alma motioned for Elmer and Joe Beck to depart. Then, staring at the cripple, she said in a loud firm voice, "He won't need you men anymore." The helpers departed, and as if on cue the crowd fell quiet; a few moments before the din was riotous, but now there was total quiet.

Alma took one step toward Uncle Joe Clemmer, and stopped. "My Goodness, if it ain't Uncle Joe" she said, smiling the gorgeous smile with the perfect teeth.

"Well you waited a long time; I heard rumors 'bout you coming for months, and here you are," Alma was still twenty feet from the crippled man.

"Uncle Joe, I want you to look at me," Sister Alma said. Joe was perpetually bent over at a 30 degree angle, but he raised his head as much as he could and managed a gap-toothed grin.

"Come over here to me, Uncle Joe," Alma said, and as she spoke the words looked out over the crowd and shouted, "Do we have any believers in this sin filled tent tonight?"

"Yes, Sister Alma, Yes," they screamed, and Alma motioned to 40A Bert, and Bert went into a low, slow rendition of "Just As I Am."

Uncle Joe Clemmer was inching over on this walking stick. Sister Alma strode over to him and leaned her 5'10" frame down to his upward turned face. All Uncle Joe could see was the deep cut cleavage of 38D's. Alma leaned in closer, almost pressing his face into the abyss, but then turned her head and whispered in his ear "Uncle Joe, how you like these big ol' titties?"

Uncle Joe jolted like electricity had gone through his body, and stood up straighter than he had in years, although he was still decidedly bent. "Think maybe that shine has kicked in," Alma thought. Everybody knew

Uncle Joe had a taste for it, and Sister Alma had instructed her faithful servant Hoover Carpenter to make sure Uncle Joe had a big long drink of it in the parking lot prior to coming in.

Alma backed up a few feet, skittering backwards on five-inch heels, curvaceous legs flexing.

"How 'bout you straighten up for Sister Alma," Alma cajoled. She turned to the crowd and said calmly, "We all try to walk the straight and narrow, right?" The crowd shouted "Yes, Sister Alma."

"Well, let's all help Uncle Joe straighten up," Alma shouted and walked back over to Uncle Joe. The crowd watched as Alma bent deeply over Uncle Joe once again, and could see his head pop up another couple inches. Pasour Rhyne had sufficiently recovered and was back in the tent. Suddenly he ran to the front, faced the group and started shouting, "Go, Uncle Joe, Go, Uncle Joe, Go, Uncle Joe." The crowd fell in like lemmings, even Uncle Joe spitting the words out as best he could.

Sister Alma leaned in again, and whispered in Uncle Joe's ear, "How would you like to put your big strong hands around these monsters," she teased, and this time Uncle Joe popped up a good 6 inches. He was getting pretty close to straight, as Hoover came up to the edge of the stage carrying a glass. Sister Alma walked over, Hoover mumbled something unintelligible, and Alma came back with the glass.

"Brothers and Sisters, Uncle Joe's throat is probably dry due to all this effort," she said holding the glass to Uncle Joe's lips. Uncle Joe drank half the glass in a gulp, thinkin' it was water. Then he really jerked and stood straight.

Sister Alma saw his movement, and looked at the audience triumphantly and pointed at Uncle Joe Clemmer, shouting "Do you see what can happen if you truly believe?"

"Yes, Sister Alma, Yes," they screamed. At this point Uncle Joe stood straighter than straight, reared his shoulders back, and started marching across the stage, Sister Alma exulting and walking alongside him, pointing at him in his glorious trek. He walked ten feet, then turned toward the crowd and tossed his walking stick toward them. Pasour Rhyne caught it in the forehead, but recovered quickly and grinned his nutty grin, then stood up and turned around and around, holding the cane in his hands and shouting, "A miracle, a miracle, a miracle." It was picked up at once, and as Uncle Joe Clemmer continued to prance across the stage, the audience screamed, "Miracle, Miracle, Miracle."

Sister Alma gave Bert a look and raised her right hand – the signal for a resounding organ moment- daaah- it went on, very loud, for ten seconds, the crowd going nuts, Uncle Joe prancing, and Sister Alma pirouetting on her 5-inch heels and shouting "Praise the Lord, Praise the Lord."

When the crescendo ended, Sister Alma walked slowly over to Uncle Joe, and put her arm around his boney shoulders, and looked at the followers. They hushed, and she said, "You have seen it, you have seen a hopeless cripple healed by the power of God, so what should you do, for the glory of God, <u>What Should You Do?</u>"

Sister Alma nodded to Bert, and she started in on "Just As I Am," and then pointed to Elmer, and he motioned for his minions to carry their collection plates through the throng.

The ushers scattered through the crowd, the mill workers and farmers holding out their paper money for collection. The Clonger bunch did fine, but Hoover Carpenter fell down twice; the parishioners were very helpful and picked him up and put back the bounty in the plate.

As Head Usher Elmer watched, for he was the overseer, he felt a pretty strong pang of guilt for ol' Pasour Rhyne; after all, he did get hit in the head with Uncle Joe's cane, and he had done a right nice job of getting' the crowd riled. Elmer caught Passour's eye, and motioned for him to come forward. Pasour came up kind of sheepishly, but when Elmer winked at him and handed him the plate, Pasour grinned that nutty grin, and when Elmerwhispered in his ear, in a weak moment, "Pinch the pot for ten bucks," Pasour took off runnin' down the aisle. Buford reflected a moment, and thought "Poor old crazy man, will prob'ly be the biggest day of his life, 'cept when he burnt down Earl Lineberger's barn."

As the ushers returned to Elmer at the front of the stage, Uncle Joe Clemmer was winding down a little, and some of his people came up and got him, and he walked away proud and erect, even doffing his straw hat to the crowd as he exited, letting out a final, "Praise the Lord and Sister Alma." Sister Alma waved to Uncle Joe and pursed her red lips, expressing a goodbye kiss.

The collection plates were overflowing, and as they came to Head Usher Elmer they dumped them into the tin tub that Sister Alma had provided. Elmer watched as each usher came up and poured the coins and bills into the big tub. Elmer thanked each usher as he left, paying special attention to Hoover, the shine purveyor.

The last to come up was Pasour Rhyne, who in addition to bringing the collection plate was leading a veal calf on a rope. "Crown Radford give us this," Pasour crowed as he poured the money into the tub.

"Take it out back and tie it to one of the tent stakes," Head Usher Elmer told him. Pasour turned to make his way out back and fell face first on the sawdust floor. He got up and had greenish looking mire on his forehead – the calf had shit while he was standing there waiting on Pasour. Pasour, ever the goofy showman, was not embarrassed at all, and turned to the crowd and delivered a final Larson-Savoney salute with a shit stained forearm. Pasour headed toward the rear of the tent, leading the veal calf and departing with a crazy giggle.

Bert hit the organ again for ten seconds, and then stopped abruptly. Then Sister Alma held her shapely arms up to the heights, and the audience was silent. Sister Alma smiled a saintly smile, an all-knowing smile and said, "Brothers and Sisters, you have seen the power of the Lord tonight, you have experienced what can happen when you believe – just ask Uncle Joe Clemmer. Ask the man who was healed in your presence, YOUR VERY PRESENCE, this evening. Now I want to send you home singing a song of thanksgiving, a song dedicated to the upcoming harvest, just around the corner."

With that Bert broke into the prelude to "Bringing in the Sheaves." Everybody knew the words by heart, and they all were on their feet, belting out the lyrics – "Bringin' in the sheaves, bringin' in the sheaves, we shall come rejoicin', bringin' in the sheaves."

Sister Alma led them in two verses and then the organ ceased abruptly. And the lights dimmed and suddenly a spotlight, which Bogus Clonger had been able to rig up at the rear of the tent, burst its bright light onto Sister Alma, encircling her in all her glory.

Sister Alma looked out at the crowd and delivered the Benediction. She always ad libbed this, for she never really knew how things were going to play out.

"Brothers and Sisters in the great family of our powerful God and his only son, Jesus Christ, our Savior, do not forget what has happened in this holy spot tonight. Never, NEVER (she shouted) forget Uncle Joe Clemmer being restored to perfect health, and never forget the love and fellowship we have enjoyed together. Remember we will have our next meeting on Friday night. And may the Lord God Almighty bless and keep you, and make your harvest a great bounty."

Sister Alma waved to the crowd, and as the lights came up, Bogus cut off the spotlight, and after a two-minute standing ovation, while Sister Alma waved and blew kisses to the crowd, the people started filing out, beaming faces of joy and chatting about the miracle they had beheld.

Chief Usher Elmer looked at the tin tub full of good old Piedmont Lint Head/Dirt farmer money and went to pick up one side.

"This thing is right heavy," he thought to himself; "lots of quarters in the bottom." Elmer looked around at the dwindling crowd for a hand; all the ushers had left, even the be-shitted Pasour Rhyne. Then he remembered seeing his brother Theodore come in late. Theodore typically had business to take care of up at Vera Pasour's house around this hour in Harden, and it had to culminate prior to her brother getting off the second shift.

"Theodore, help me carry this back to Sister Alma's dressing room; you can help me count it if you want to."

Theodore grunted and took one side of the tub. He and Elmer usually got along well, but since Elmer had become Chief Usher and Bert the organist, seemed to him that Elmer had gotten a case of the big head.

Plus Elmer thought he had a chance with Sister Alma; but Theodore knew better than that. Theodore was satisfied he would be getting' some of that soon. "Shit, I know that ham I give her sealed the deal," he thought, and a smile crossed his lips as they carried the tub into the dressing room.

"Well here it is," said Elmer, as Alma clucked about the bounty. "Nigger John offered a big bag of fried chicken and chitterlings, but I told him nice like to take it on home; tol' him to bring you a watermelon when they come in season."

Sister Alma nodded in agreement. She did not discriminate; she would take gifts from any color or creed – but she did have her limits.

"That's good, Elmer, ain't been able to stomach chitlins since that time I found a corn kernel and a butterbean in one. Just gives me the creeps now," she said.

"Elmer, since it is so late, how 'bout ya'll put that tub in the trunk of my car and call it a night," she said, handing the keys to the black Cadillac to Chief Usher Elmer.

Sister Alma followed the brothers out to the now nearly empty parking lot; when Elmer wasn't looking she brushed her bounteous breasts against Theodore's elbow then did the same to Elmer when Theodore didn't see. Both actions got the desired reaction as the fair-skinned red-headed siblings turned crimson.

After they put the tub in the trunk she told them goodnight and Elmer and Theodore trudged to their cars, off to delight in their individual fantasies.

When they were gone a tall man emerged from the shadows and was greeted with a beautiful smile and a long, deep kiss. It was Polie Maxwell, Mayor of Dallas. He stood 6'3" and the women said he was good lookin'. Bert the organist put him in a league with Ned Cannon, purported to be the handsomest man in Stanley. As they released from the embrace Polie said, "Let's go get something to eat; I got a quart of shine from Oodley Creek."

"Let's go lover "Alma cooed, and grabbed Polie's tight ass as they got in the car.

Sister Alma — Part II

Dr. Fesperman turned to Sister Alma and shook his head. "No doubt about it, Alma, I'd say you are about two months along." The doctor was short and stocky and was always in a three-piece suit.

"Okay Doctor, guess I'll just have to deal with it." She looked hard at him and opened her blouse, loosening her bra.

"These have been a little sensitive lately; could you examine them?" Her lips were pouty as the good doctor grasped the 38Ds with both hands, kneading and pulling. Alma sat quietly as he finished. "Feel okay, in my professional opinion," he grinned. "How much do I owe you Doctor," Alma cooed as she hiked up her bounty and corralled them.

"Not a thing honey," Dr. Fesperman chuckled. He was known for his good humor and willingness to take things in trade – bartering he called it.

"But I'll tell you something, Alma. I have received as much as two Rhode Island Red laying hens for a thorough breast exam."

Alma turned to leave, shaking her curvy bottom at him and said with a smile, "You oughta be payin' me." Dr. Fesperman cackled and with a resounding whack on her fine ass sent her on her way.

Alma walked across the gravel parking lot to the Buick, where Polie Maxwell was sitting, smoking a cigar and drinking a Falstaff beer.

"Well, it's official now," Alma told Polie. Polie looked more than a little peaked, kind of like he might throw up.

"Wha, wha, what are we gonna do Alma, you know I'm trapped. If my daddy-in-law found out about this I'd never get another red cent, and my political future would be in the can and ——"

"Damn, Polie, quit your blubbering; a hell of a lot of good your incessant whining is gonna do. Besides, I've got a plan I think will work, and if it does, you'll be off the hook and I'll be a saint. Let me work on it awhile, then I'll clue you in."

Alma had her Concordance out, checking the facts. "It's gotta be here early in the New Testament," she ruminated, turning the Concordance to the verse for virgin birth." Matthew, Chapter 1," she cried triumphantly. Let's see now, verse 18, if I leave out the early part of the verse and pick up with 'before they came together, she was found with child of the Holy Ghost.'" Alma felt like she was on the right track.

"I am just going to have to pick and choose carefully, not mention anything about Jesus," certainly not indicate anything relative to the sex of her unborn child – for of course she didn't know.

"Yes," she thought, "then in verse 20 it says 'the angel of the Lord appeared. . . . for that which is conceived in her is of the Holy Ghost,'" Alma read further.

"I will just have to edit out any references to the sex of the child and totally concentrate on the concept of the virgin birth," Sister Alma thought.

"Here it is, verse 23," Alma exulted to herself. "Behold, a virgin shall be with child," she read, noting not to include the remainder of the verse which referenced bringing forth a son.

"Just gonna have to be real careful with my words, concentrate on parts of verses, and lay it on heavy, super heavy, with the virgin birth stuff," Sister Alma said out loud to herself.

"Yes," she thought, 'Immaculate Conception' they call it. Guess there will just have to be room for one more. Move over Mary, Sister Alma is coming through."

THE PROPHET EZEKIEL

With that Alma closed her seldom-used Bible. She had a lot of thinking to do; tomorrow night was tent meeting and she had to get her ducks in a row for the announcement. It was going to be a bang up meeting on Wednesday.

Russ finished off the last of the potatoes on his plate and drank down the half glass of buttermilk remaining. Granny and little Lois had finished supper and were sitting out on the front porch. Russ had been a little late coming home; they were shorthanded since Thomas had quit.

"What made ol' Thomas quit?" Sarah asked, lookin' a little funny at Russ.

"Oh, I dunno," he said, "He was sort of an oddball and never really fit in. You know he was some of that Lingerfelt trash over near Double Shoals, and he wa'n't much of a worker."

Double Shoals was thus named because there were two shoals 'bout a hundred yards apart there on the South Fork River; there was a cotton mill on the bank that employed a good many Gaston County lint heads – that being the moniker for cotton mill workers.
"Yes, he never really fit in, even Nigger John didn't like him – Charles was a misfit and we won't miss him," Russ said.

Sarah looked at Monk, short for Monkey (her pet name for him because of all his antics) but didn't say a word; however, she did remember Russ mentioning Charles beggin' tobacco, and she had noticed that the tin of red pepper had miraculously reappeared in the cabinet. "Don't think I'll scratch that one," she thought to herself, and asked Russ if he wanted some chocolate pie or a stickie for dessert.

"No Red," he replied, "you know I ate that half a peach pie you sent with me for lunch. Mighty good, can't beat them Georgia Belles," he exclaimed.

Sarah sat down at the table beside Russ and rubbed him hard on the top of his head. A good head rubbin' was one of the things he really loved;

25

another one was getting' up against the door opening and rubbin' his back against it really hard. He would groan with joy and Sarah and Lois, and Granny if she was around, would giggle at his antics. He was a clown at heart, and a very good-natured one at that.

"You know Red, we ain't been out anywhere for a while. I was thinkin' maybe we could go out for a while tonight – just for a little bit."

Sarah looked at him and wiped the remainder of cornbread and milk from her mouth and asked, "Well I'll Swannee, that might be alright; I bet Granny wouldn't mind, for she could take care of Lois."

"I don't think we even need to ask Granny to babysit, 'cause Lois can go with us. I was thinkin' that maybe, just for entertainment, we could ride down to Sister Alma's tent meeting. You know Elmer and Bert will be there of course, so Lois and Nan can play together. Whatcha think?"

Sarah's eyes brightened. "Let's do it; be real interestin' to see if she says anything 'bout Uncle Joe Clemmer. That cure he got two months ago put him in the bed for two weeks – everybody knows it. Wonder how she would explain that away?"

"Well, I know what Elmer said about it," said Russ. "He said Sister Alma figgered he got some kind of moonshine poisoning, and that's what laid him up. Elmer and Bert both swear to it. Claim some shine Hoover Carpenter gave him out in the parking lot before the service did it."

"Reckon Sister Alma didn't know nothin' 'bout that," Red said, grinning at the Monkey.

"That's the word," he said. "Let's wash up a little and go see the show."

"Deal," said Red.

Alma looked at the plain white dress. It came below the knee and rode up high in the front.

"Pure white," she mused, wondering how the men in the crowd would react to the very obvious absence of cleavage.

"Virginal," she thought, and picked her plain flats out of the closet floor. "No flash for this announcement," Alma said out loud. "The flash will be in the words," she shouted in her bedroom. Alma would often speak out loud when she was alone in her house, particularly if she were preparing for a special healing session, or love offering (she'd truly LOVED those) or a momentous announcement. Her news to share with the parishioners this lovely evening would definitely cause an upheaval of Biblical proportions – she was satisfied of that.

"Gonna be the delivery, and the right words, and I think I've got 'em both," she nearly shouted, feeling the fire building in her.

Alma knew she needed to settle herself down a little; it was only four in the afternoon and the tent meeting was three and a half hours off. She poured half a glass of Oodley Creek shine into a tumbler and took a few sips. Just then there was a knock on her front door and dressed in her robe she went to answer it. She knew who it was, for it was time to set things in motion, time to orchestrate. "Like a God damned Broadway play," she said to herself as she opened the front door to see Head Usher Elmer standing there in a rather tight pinstriped suit. Alma had told him tonight was the very most special night in the history of her crusade and that he needed to wear his very best.

"He-hello Miss Alma," Elmer stammered when she opened the door. He looked at her in her robe, wondering how much was under there, or not.

"Come in Elmer; my you are my timely man," Alma cooed, grasping Elmer's big arm and leading him into the living room.

"Have a seat on the sofa, Elmer and I'll be right back." Elmer sat down, his tight britches riding up in the crotch a mite. Alma walked into the bedroom and brought out a glass of Oodley Creek's finest and handed it to Elmer. He took the drink and watched, holding his breath, as Sister Alma slid onto the sofa beside him.

"My God," Elmer thought, as Alma sat within six inches of him and started rubbing her shoulder, the robe sliding a little, as the front opened slightly.

"Like the parting of the Red Sea," he thought, as Alma fiddled with her robe, pretending to close it but actually opening the front more so that Elmer would have something to see.

"You know Elmer, I asked you over here to go over the schedule for tonight, 'cause this is gonna be the biggest night ever in Dallas – actually the biggest ever in Gaston County. And I wanted you to know about it before anybody else, because you have been such a faithful supporter, not to mention your dear wife Bert, my wonderful organist." As Alma finished saying this she took her right hand and kind of positioned her left breast to a little more exposed position, pushing her tongue between her lips.

"Ye-yep, Sister Alma, I knew it must be important to get me over here." Elmer's head was in a whirl; in fact, when Alma had mentioned Bert his first thought was "Bert who."

"Well, Elmer, a fantastic and other-worldly event is going to occur, right here in Dallas, NC."

Alma looked at Elmer earnestly, and he looked back, as much as he dared, his eyes continually traveling back to the partially opened robe.

"Elmer, you know the story of Mary in the Bible, and how she gave birth to little baby Jesus without ever having, you know, been with a man. Her mate was Joseph but they had never so to speak, had relations."

Elmer nodded dutifully, not quite sure where this was going. He had a vague recollection of the story Alma was talking about, but had never really considered the sexual mechanics of the thing. "Right interesting concept," he thought to himself, "getting' a youngun' without screwing." Elmer made a mental note to do some extensive pondering on the subject later.

Sister Alma looked at Elmer and continued. "It's all there in the first chapter of Matthew, in the marvelous New Testament, which exists only to glorify the life and times and preaching and miracles of our sweet Lord Jesus Christ."

Sister Alma's voice had been rising and she leaped to her feet and turned her back to Buford, and as she did she dropped the robe.

Elmer swallowed his snuff and had to take a big drink of Oodley Creek shine to keep from choking. Alma turned to Elmer and looked at him hard. She placed the palms of her hands on her belly.

"There is a baby in here, Elmer, and you know I have never been with a man in my life – you do know that – right, Elmer?," Alma entreated. Buford did not know what to look at first, so he just looked at everything, for a good minute, taking in the full Alma exposure.

Elmer felt a little light-headed, part from the snuff and part from the circumstances.

Alma turned her back to Elmer and bent over to pick up her robe. Elmer got his last look, a lengthy one as Alma was bent over a good twenty seconds.

Sister Alma came back over to the sofa, now wrapped tightly in her robe and sat down beside Elmer, not so close this time.

"It's called 'immaculate conception,' just like with the Virgin Mary, 'cept this time it's the Virgin Alma. I know it is difficult to understand, but an angel appeared before me the other month and told me what was going to happen. Yes, I am going to give birth to a child of God. Yep 'immaculate conception,' just like in the Bible with the Virgin Mary, but now it is the Virgin Alma. You do understand, don't you, how it is such an incredible honor to be so chosen?"

Elmer was having a little trouble keeping his lunch down after the snuff ordeal, but he had followed what Sister Alma had said. He could only nod politely.

"Now, Elmer, I have been chosen, and in turn, because of your undying faithfulness and devotion to the ministry I am choosing YOU."

Alma's voice rose on the YOU and Elmer shifted his feet nervously. "When someone is talking about being pregnant and says somethin' 'bout choosing YOU, ain't no good can come of it," he thought, but continued to listen.

"YOU, Elmer, I need YOU to help spread the word, the fabulous news of Immaculate Conception. Ya see, this is such an unusual occurrence, why only twice in the history of the world, that I fear that if I announced it all of a sudden from the stage it would be too great a shock, so I want you to clue in the ushers and have them mention the pending Virgin Birth to some of the community leaders as they come in. Tell them to say Sister Alma will make the official announcement tonight."

"Yes, Sister Alma," said Elmer. Elmer decided not to think too hard 'bout this "truncated perception" concept until he had more time for private cogitating; it didn't matter too much anyway, for he trusted and believed in Sister Alma and would do anything she said.

"Yes, Sister Alma," he repeated again as he got up to leave. He was almost to the door when Alma stopped him.

"And Elmer, let's leave Pasour Rhyne and Hoover out of this loop, as far as spreading the word; I just don't think their credibility is up to snuff."

"Yes, Sister Alma," Elmer said as he went out the door, wishing that Alma had not used the word snuff.

It was close to camp meeting time; Elmer had driven home and sat in the back yard under the black walnut tree for a good hour thinking about what Sister Alma had told him and trying to settle himself down in the belly with a glass of buttermilk. He was trying to come to grips with the "Virgin Birth" issue and not making too much progress; every time he thought he was kinda startin' to understand it he remembered the unadorned Alma standing in front of him, and then bending over in front of him.

"My God," he thought, "I guess anything is possible if a poor country boy like me can see a sight like her, naked as a jaybird." Somehow it made the virgin birth idea more believable.

Elmer finished the buttermilk and went on in the house. Bert and Nan would be 'bout ready to go, and he didn't want to be late. There was a lot of prompting to be done with the ushers, so he would need extra time for that.

The throng was beginning to arrive and as usual the ushers came down front to where Elmer was to give instructions. Elmer was fumbling with a piece of paper on which was written in Sister Alma's flowing script in capital letters IMMACULATE CONCEPTION. He had had to go check with her at her little dressing room about the exact words. Alma had been dressed in her modest pure white dress, makeup toned down considerably. She had written down the two words for Buford, then put her arm in his and looked at him hard.

"Tonight is the biggest night of our lives; now get those ushers up to speed on what to say," she had told him.

Elmer sized up who he had tonight as he fingered the magic words. There was Bogus Clonger, Preacher Clonger, Joe Beck, and his brother Theodore. Pasour Rhyne and Hoover Carpenter were present but ignored.

Once Elmer had their attention he began. "Now all you faithful ushers, you know how wonderful Sister Alma has been to us, and the many blessings she has bestowed upon us through her ministry, RIGHT?"

"Yes, yes Elmer," they said as one.

"Well faithful ushers, it is time for us to give back to Sister Alma, to return a small portion of faith and devotion that she has given us for so long, RIGHT?"

"Yes, yes, Elmer," they said again. Elmer was silent for a good twenty seconds, and just looked at the ushers. Alma had mentioned that this might be a good thing, taking a page from her own drama book.

Elmer began again. "Now boys, you know how Sister Alma has performed so many miracles and good deeds for the community; now is the time for us to return the favor. Like when she cured Uncle Joe Clemmer, did we doubt her then?"

"No, Elmer," they said.

"Well now she has asked us to have faith in her again, for a most wondrous thing has occurred; now you all would agree that you know that Sister Alma has never been with a man – I know there were rumors one time but we all know it was the Devil's Work. Right?"

The ushers looked at each other sheepishly, but eventually said, "Yes, Elmer, we know that to be true."

"Well, a miracle has happened, and Sister Alma has been visited by an angel, and the Holy Ghost has come to be inside her, and at this very moment she is carrying a child of God inside her."

Deafening silence from the ushers.

"I am telling you it is true, it is all in the first chapter of the New Testament, Matthew, so you know it has got to be true. It is called the Virgin Birth, like with Mary and Jesus. It is called IMMACULATE CONCEPTION."

At this the ushers were still silent, until Theodore said, "Yep, Elmer, I do remember that, 'smattersfact it is also in the book of Revolutions, just read it the other night when I was doin' my Bible study."

Theodore didn't usher all that much, but he was respected by all the ushers; he had once been a constable and had packed a sidearm in his duties.

"Come to think of it, I believe I heard the preacher over at Harden talk about that; fact is, I'm sure I did," said Joe Beck Clonger. Joe Beck was also well respected; he ran a store and garage up at Costner in a building he rented from Beeler Froneberger.

After Joe Beck said his piece, coupled with the endorsement from Theodore, the ushers mumbled their allegiance to the IMMACULATE CONCEPTION idea. The deal was sealed when T.G. "Preacher" Clonger said "Well, Sister Alma ain't never steered us wrong, so if she said it it must be true."

Elmer beamed, and instructed the ushers what to say to the community leaders as they showed them to their seats.

"<u>And say it like you mean it</u>," Elmer decreed as the emboldened ushers headed off to work.

Elmer reflected a moment, thinkin' bout how things had come together, and he thought about how as a child and young man he had been <u>soooo</u> petrified to speak in front of a group. He made a mental note to relate this speech to Sister Alma; he knew she would be proud of him.

"Especially that twenty second 'pregnant pause,'" he thought, then reconsidered the verbiage.

Preacher Clonger was greeting Clarence and Ila Thornburg and ushering them to their seats. They were not really local dignitaries, the ones that Alma wanted to be alerted to "Immaculate Conception," and they actually weren't even local, living up near Lincolnton - pronounced "Lankern" by the locals. Ila was a sister to Russ, Elmer, and Theodore. But Preacher thought he would get in a little practice. He cleared his throat and said "Welcome to the revival, Clarence and Ila; good to see ya, and I want to tell you that tonight is a very special night and that Sister Alma is going to announce that she is with child, having been visited by The Holy Ghost."

Ila had just put in a dip of Railroad Mills snuff and she dern near swallowed it, but managed to gain control. "Okay," Ila croaked; she really had no idea what he was jabbering about, but thought better of making a comment. Her husband Clarence just looked at Preacher with his big ol' googly eyes with the coke bottle lenses in front of them.

"Yep," said Preacher, "It's called "Innoculated Perception," and this is only the second time it has ever happened in the known history of the world, even before Columbus." Ila and Clarence just looked at him blankly.

Preacher thought to himself that it went pretty good for a first try. "Believe I got them big words down now," he mused as he went on with his ushering.

Usher Bogus Clonger had picked out an actual dignitary to start with, none other than Mayor Polie Maxwell, who had just come into the main area of the tent from the rear, over where Sister Alma's little dressing room was.

"Welcome, Mayor Maxwell," Bogus caroled, remembering to wipe his Red Man tobacco stained chin before he proffered his right hand to His Honor. Polie squeezed Bogus' hand, noticing it was kinda small, then remembering the missing fingers from the planing affair.

"Good to see you Bogus, I hope we'll have another oyster roast benefit out at your place this fall. You know election time is not far off, and I am certain you good Democrats are ready to get goin' on a rally."

Bogus beamed a big ol' Democrat smile and said "Yessir, Mayor, we will surely do it. You know tonight is a very special night and Sister Alma is going to announce that she is with child, the father being the Holy Ghost, who visited her a coupla months ago after an angel told her it was gonna happen."

Mayor Maxwell looked at Bogus carefully and said "Well My, that certainly is big news, but remember that miracles have happened before – why what about Jesus Christ?"

Bogus' eyes got big as he exclaimed, "Why Mayor, you are right on it; this will only be the second time in the history of the world. And ya' know what it's called?" Bogus said.

"Well no, I don't believe I do," replied Polie Maxwell. Polie could be rather coy when he wanted to, and he figgered now was a very good time.

"It's 'Immersion Menstruation," shouted Bogus, feeling proud that his pronunciation was on line.

Polie Maxwell stifled a chuckle, and gave Bogus a big bear hug. "Thanks Bogus," he said. "I 'preciate it and we'll get together this fall, alright?"

Bogus grinned his big ol' 'backer stained grin and waved wildly as the mayor went to his seat. Polie smiled and thought "Just might work after all."

Sister Alma was putting the final touches on her toned-down makeup – very light rouge, just a hint of lipstick, and very faint eyeliner. The push up bra had been eschewed for a simple white 38 D. The white was perfect with her virginal white, plain dress. One last look in the mirror hanging off the wire in her little makeshift dressing room and she deemed herself to be ready.

"Remember," she told herself, "keep away from Jesus and Mary, accentuate the virgin birth, throw in the edited Matthew stuff, sling it against the wall and see if it sticks." Sister Alma had a lot of confidence in the gullibility of the people of the greater Dallas area, and the moment of truth, rather believability, was at hand. With a deep breath she strode through the opening in the curtain and headed to the stage.

As she came into view of the crowed, the biggest ever, Bert lit into "How Great Thou Art." Alma thought this would be a nice touch. "Well, Virgin Birth ought to indicate an air of greatness," Alma said to herself as she mounted the steps to the stage.

It was the quietest she could ever recollect for an entrance, but that could be good – or not. The lights had been lowered as Alma had prescribed, but as she reached the middle of the stage the bright spear of the spotlight hit her. Bogus Clonger had been able to rig up the light once again. On cue, Bert stopped the music the moment the light came on. Sister Alma stood in the stark yellow light and looked from one side of the gathering to the other – twice. Then she began.

"Brothers and Sisters in the legion of the Holy Ghost; I know many of you have been told a little bit about what I have to announce, but some of you don't know. Let me ask you this, have I ever steered you wrong?"

A low rumbling unison of "No, Sister Alma," could be heard. Sister Alma looked at the crowd, her lovely eyes moving from left to right.

"Well if we agree on that, why would I start now, why would I try to deceive you when such an incredible miracle has occurred. Would Sister Alma do that to you?" she called out.

"No, Sister Alma," reverberated from the seats, a little stronger than the first response.

Alma paused for a good twenty seconds and looked at the audience. Chief Usher Elmer was watching intently, and battling back the recollection of his thinking of the phrase "pregnant pause," although he couldn't help but grin inwardly at his cleverness.

"Children, two months ago I was visited by an Angel from God. I know I did not tell any of you about this event; please forgive me, but I was so overwhelmed that I could not act. But the angel of the Lord told me that I was going to receive a great gift from the Holy Ghost. Do you hear what I am saying, Children of God? I am saying that just like it says in the first chapter of our beloved New Testament, that an angel visits, and then the woman bears the child of the Holy Ghost. We are talkin' 'Virgin Birth' here, and it is going to happen. Yes, I have been chosen by God and through this magical intervention I am now with child, a child of God."

Sister Alma stood stock still, and for one of the first times in her years of tending to the faithful flock was at a loss for words. Fortunately it was momentary.

Then she lit into the clincher, "Children, do you have faith in me?" Alma said.

"Yes Sister Alma," they said, a little stronger.

"Can anybody say Amen?" she asked. A deep baritone amen came from the direction of the Honorable Mayor, followed by a chorus of others.

Alma felt it building.

"Faith," she shouted, "faith, faith, faith. You gotta believe, it is all in the first chapter of Matthew, it was Jesus and Mary; you know the story. It has come to pass once again. Who can say it is untrue? Who can deny the Scripture? FAITH, FAITH. Don't you see things every day that you don't understand, children?"

"Yes, Sister Alma," they said.

"Okay," said Sister Alma, "somebody stand up and tell me how electricity works."

She watched as the group looked at each other kind of embarrassedly.

"Well, we use it every day, but nobody has a clue as to how it works. RIGHT?" She shouted this out.

The crowd got a little excited, some exclaiming, "That's right, That's right," and others just saying "Yes, Sister Alma," and looking like they were on the verge of a revelation.

"When you flip that switch, you have FAITH (and she shouted it again) that the light will come on. RIGHT?"

"Yes, Sister Alma, Yes" they joined in.

Alma stood still again and looked out over the crowd. Time for the kill.

"Tonight, I am proclaiming to you my friends and faithful parishioners, my Holy Pregnancy, and I want you all to stand up and shout "Hallelujah, Sister Alma."

"Yes, Sister Alma," they shouted, then on cue, with perfect timing, 40A Bert hit the organ hard and started in on "Just as I am." The followers rose as one and Sister Alma led them – "Just as I am, without one plea ——-"

Alma belted out the words and the crowd's communal voice grew stronger toward the end, and some of the faithful began to jump up and put their hands toward the sky, 'til more than half of them were jumping and shouting and Bert, as planned, abruptly ceased the organ playing. And on cue, Bogus cut the spot light and the house lights came on, Head Usher Elmer at the switch.

Sister Alma looked out at her flock, and said "I know you have never seen anything like this before, RIGHT?" and she shouted the last word.

"Yes, Sister Alma" they bellowed, and she knew she had them.

She went on – "Well I want you to know that I will keep on preaching, and that because you are all in my family of the Holy Ghost, I will give you constant updates on the progress of the Divine Pregnancy – and I don't want you to worry, for I will not abandon you in this time, and our meetings will go on as scheduled, for this wonderful gift I have received must be shared with you, brothers and sisters." At that moment the Bogus operated spotlight came back on and the house lights were doused.

"What a well-oiled machine I have created," Alma thought to herself, just as Bert began "Bringing in the sheaves, bringing in the sheaves, we will come rejoicing, bringing in the sheaves, bringing in the sheaves, bringing in the sheaves, we will come rejoicing, bringing in – the sheaves."

Alma was leading the singing with her strong soprano, and the crowd thundered along with her. She slowed the ending down and they went right with it, "bringing innnn, the sheaves."

The followers then erupted with shouts of "praise the Lord" and "Virgin Birth." Pasour Rhyne jumped up in front of the group and started shouting "Emancipation Proclamation," while doing the Larson Savoney sign over and over. Everybody knew Pasour was a nut but the machine was rolling, and they continued to shout and exult.

Alma waited for the organ to cease and looked at the group, really hard. I mean really hard. A quiet came over them and she began her closing.

"Brothers and sisters in God and the Holy Ghost, go forth, and never forget what you have heard, the miracle that has been revealed. Now let us pray." All the brothers and sisters bowed their heads as one as she began.

"Dear God and bountiful Holy Ghost, watch over these faithful, and restore them daily in the knowledge and faith in what they have heard this blessed evening. In the name of the Holy Ghost and our Lord, Amen."

Bogus cut the light and the house lights came up, and Alma solemnly left the stage. Near the rear of the tent Russ and Sarah looked at each other. Rus winked at Sarah and said, "Well, Red, guess we have just witnessed a true miracle." Sarah chuckled, shook her head, and said "let's get little Lois and head to the house, Monk."

Sister Alma — Part III

Sister Alma was in her bedroom, turned sideways in front of the full-length mirror, one of the nice oval ones that swiveled and had oak trim and beveled glass.

She was wearing a nightgown and placing one arm above and one arm below her large protrusion.

"It's gettin' out there," she said out loud. "Of course it should be out there," she thought, "'cause it is 8 ½ months along accordin' to the good Dr. Fesperman."

Alma chuckled to herself when she thought about her visits to the doctor's office during her pregnancy, and how she would always "work a deal" and doc would always "work a barter." Alma felt like both parties always wound up happy; Dr. Fesperman always had that impish look in his eye as Alma left, and Alma always gave her now "more than ample" tail an extra shake as she went out the door. Alma could hear the doctor cackling as she went down the hall. She thought back to this last visit, when Polie Maxwell was waiting out in the big Buick drinkin' a Falstaff beer. He lit his dormant cigar as Alma slid in beside him.

"So how's the Child of the Holy Ghost comin' along," he grinned and handed Alma a beer.

"Just fine," she said, "as is the Holy Virgin Mother. The doctor thinks it is going to be a girl, the way the baby is laying in there. He says it could be anytime."

Polie Maxwell beamed a giant smile; he had warmed to this fatherhood role since it had become quite apparent that the good gullible folks of Dallas had bought into the Virgin Birth concept, and that nothing was required of him.

"Dr. Fesperman says I am doin' fine also, though he did say that I had gained a little more weight than he thought was good," she said.

Ever since the announcement of the Virgin Birth six months ago the faithful had insisted on a weekly "Blessed Child of the Holy Ghost" love offering. This additional stipend allowed Sister Alma to eat even higher on the hog than before; there was a French restaurant in Charlotte that she loved, and Polie carried her over there at least once a week. That tab and her skyrocketing Scotch bill pretty much depleted the baby love offering, but it was replenished like clockwork each week.

Sister Alma reflected on the past six months as Polie Maxwell drove her home. She had been able to do about like before, camp meetings at least twice a week. The crowd had actually increased as news of the "immaculate conception" spread. Alma was even getting some people from across the Catawba River near Charlotte, and others from Lincolnton. Alma had told Dr. Fesperman to spread the word, but she had no idea he would.

That old bird can surprise you," she chuckled, remembering how he insisted on very thorough breast examinations at each visit.

"You can't be too thorough," he always said, "You know I am a Scorpio." The doctor would say this and give his cackly laugh.

Alma thought of all these things as she gazed at herself in the oval. She was fascinated by her "big bump," and was beginning to get excited about the imminent birth.

Russ pushed back from the table and rubbed his belly. He had just finished off two fried pies, one peach and one apple. It was late January, so of course the fruit was out of season, but it was dried fruit. Every summer the peaches and apples Sarah didn't can were dried. The process was not complicated; you peeled and sliced the fruit and then let it dry in the sun over several days. Sarah liked to put a sheet up on top of the low-pitched smokehouse roof and dry them there. Little Lois could handle this, so she would give her a sheet and tell her to spread it out on the smokehouse roof, and then send her up there with buckets of the fruit to spread out in the sun. It was not a hard job, and Little Lois would jump right on it.

That's how you had fried fruit pies in the middle of the winter. Sarah made them the way Granny had showed her; roll out the dough, cut a circle about six inches across (Luzianne Coffee cans did well) and put the fruit filling on one half of the circle. Then you flipped the empty side over and crimped the edge with a fork. Throw it in the hot lard in a frying pan and there you go. Red liked making them 'cause Little Lois and Granny, and of course Monk, loved them. She even liked them herself, and always made extra so Monk could carry them to work for lunch.

"Well they say Sister Alma's baby is 'bout due," said Russ looking around the table at the rest of them.

"Well I'll Swanney," said Granny. "I jest don't know what to think of all them goin's on down there at Dallas. I know Elmer and Bert believe in it so strong, but sometimes I wonder if that woman is just hoo-dooing everybody in the name of the Lord."

Sarah looked at Granny, and Red's eyes got kind of big. She had never heard Granny say anything quite like this in referring to Sister Alma. She kind of figgered Granny must have been holding her tongue in deference to Elmer and Bert.

Granny gave a sad sigh, so Sarah said "Now Granny, I know what you are saying but if you say anything like that to them you can't win – I am sure they are gonna believe what they want."

"That's true, what Sarah said, Mom, maybe we just oughta not say too much about it. It would probly hurt their feelins something awful."

"Reckon y'all are right," Granny said, letting out another sigh. "You know that ol' song 'Farther along we'll know all about it, farther along we'll understand why".....

Russ thought maybe it was a good time for a change of topic. "Well, we need to get some good sleep tonight, for as you know tomorrow is hog-killin' day. Gonna be a good one for it – high of 35 degrees."

Russ was grinning and looking at Sarah; he knew she would work as hard as anyone else, but he also knew how bad she hated the whole process. Sarah paid him no mind and said not to worry, she would be up early, ready to go.

"Yep, Ellis Clonger is gonna help me with the whole thing, startin' with puttin' down that big Poland-China hog. We're gonna have us some meat this year."

Russ had done well with this hog, and inexpensively; he had let the hog stay in the woods all fall and it had got big and fat eating chestnuts.

"I got the block and tackle out there ready so we can string him up, and the big wheelbarrow is there to catch the guts when we cut him open. Course that'll be after he's scalded and scraped."

"Are you gonna clean up some innards for chitterlings?" Granny asked, her eyes gleaming behind the thick wire rimmed eyeglasses.

"Sure Granny, we'll sling you some out and clean 'em real good – We'll shoot the hose pipe through 'em."

Monk was watching Red as he was talking and noticed that little involuntary gulp she gave. "Member that time at Homecoming at Lander's Chapel when Preacher Krummitt bit down on a chitlin' and found three kernels of corn in it?" Russ slapped his thigh and laughed. "You have never seen such spittin' and carrying on; Burton Payseur said he thought he heard the Preacher say a Sunday school word."

Sarah bolted from the kitchen and headed for the general direction of the outhouse. Russ grinned at Granny, who was still laughing softly.

"She'll be better tomorrow night, after it's all over," he said, and walked out into the cold air to bring in wood to fill up the box. He heard some hacking and spitting coming from the outhouse. "Some things never change," he said, grinning, and filled his arms with the red oak pieces.

Elmer was back in front of the long mirror in his bedroom; he was practicing, staring so hard into the reflection like he could see through it.

"Now brothers and sisters in Christ, let us . . . .

"No," he thought, "that won't work," remembering that Christ was out and the Holy Ghost was in.

"We need to constantly remind these people who planted this burgeoning seed in my belly," Sister Alma had told Elmer.

Having realized his error Elmer began again, "Now Brothers and Sisters in the wonderful spirit of the Duet of the Holy Ghost and Sister Alma, and in honor of the pending birth of the child of the' Immaculate Conception,' please now open up your hearts and pocket books to honor the future of the Holy Child. As you know all the monies from these special love offerings are being handled by our esteemed Mayor Polie Maxwell, and will go toward the religious education of this wondrous child of God, who will be born very soon."

"Like it," thought Elmer, and decided to go with it verbatim. As Sister Alma had progressed in her holy pregnancy she had decided to delegate some of the duties, like the prayer of preparation for the Love Offering for the Baby of the Holy Ghost. Of course Chief Usher Elmer came to mind first, so Alma counseled with Elmer about his delivery, not to mention Jesus, lay it on heavy with the Holy Ghost, and other such suggestions as she might come up with.

Elmer had gotten off to a kinda rough start in his first attempt several months earlier. When he had gotten up on the stage in front of the throng he had felt his knees start to shake and then his throat dry up.

"Brothers and Sisters," he had begun with a croak, "let us now turn our attention and bountiful gifts toward the child of the Emancipation Proclamation." The crowd got deathly quiet and Chief Usher Elmer bolted from the stage. He walked behind the stage where he could be by himself and collect his thoughts.

"God Dern idiot Pasour Rhyne, now he's got me sayin' it," he thought, ruing the day he had met the Larson Savoney nut. Elmer had stayed back there until the camp meeting was over and Sister Alma came back to talk to him. Elmer knew she would.

Alma walked up to Elmer, put her hand under his downcast chin and pulled it level.

"Why Elmer, you gonna let a little stage fright stop you?" she asked, giving him a penetrating stare, one she usually reserved for a healing session.

"I guess I just got scared," he blubbered. "Ya know, chief ushering is one thing but talking in front of all them people is sumpin' else. Mebbe you oughta get somebody else, someone who can handle it," Elmer said.

Alma ramped up the hard look a notch and reached up and put her right hand on Elmer's left cheek, and slowly and softly caressed the ruddy skin; she moved her hand delicately.

Chief Usher Elmer felt like a hot water faucet had just been plugged into his body; an overpowering warmth coursed through him.

Elmer had never felt a touch so full of love, and he turned to Alma ready for orders.

Sister Alma saw his resolve return. She reached up, pulled Elmer's head down between her now mountainous breasts, and then gave him a resounding kiss on the cheek.

"You will be fine, Elmer, just practice in front of your tall mirror and you will be fine," Alma told him.

Chief Usher Elmer took this advice to heart and he came to be at ease in front of the crowd, but he would always run through it in front of the mirror before camp meeting night. Elmer decided he had practiced enough and went out into the kitchen where Bert was sorting through her music.

"Sister Alma wants to kinda change the songs we do to a more upbeat sound," Bert said, pulling her stocking up above the knee on the tree trunk and tying a knot in it. Bert recited the songs Alma wanted her to play: O for a Thousand Tongues to Sing, How Great Thou Art (for healing sessions), For the Beauty of the Earth (Alma felt this a good generic one, no mention of Jesus – don't need references to any OTHER virgin births-, Joyful, Joyful We Adore Thee (another healing night one) and the clincher, from Page 132 of the Methodist Hymnal, Holy Ghost, Dispel Our Sadness.

"This Holy Ghost song is something Sister Alma is particularly partial to," said Bert. "She says it is a real good tie in to the Virgin Birth and Immaculate Conception. Don't ya think so, Elmer?" she asked.

"Sure," Elmer grunted. He was reciting his preparatory prayer in his mind.

"Oh yeah, Elmer, almost forgot, Sister Alma wants to include little Nan in the service in some way; she thinks it will help get people more in the mood to receive the holy baby, if we kind of put a child in the forefront. Dontcha think?"

Elmer was fantasizing about how Sister Alma had pulled his head down and stroked his cheek and kissed him.

"Sure," he said, "I'll do whatever she says." Bert seemed okay with that answer and gathered up her songs and went into the kitchen so she could check them out while she worked on supper.

Elmer went into the living room and noticed the fire was out in the potbellied stove. He went out to the back porch where he kept kerosene in a glass gallon jug and returned with a cupful. He tossed it on the wood and struck a kitchen match against the side of the stove and tossed it inside. The inside of the stove roared to life, and it reminded Oscar of how Roy Clonger had picked up the wrong bottle and put gasoline on embers; it exploded and Roy wound up dying after gettin' pneumonia.

"Course they were tired, taking care of sick kids, but what a horrible mistake," he thought, remembering that Roy was Sarah's brother-in-law.

Elmer sat down in his favorite chair. He liked to think when he was in this chair, especially if he was alone, and he felt like he had some thinkin' to do.

Elmer started thinking about mistakes, and about fire. "There could be a parallel here," he thought to himself. The word parallel was one he had learned recently, and he thought this situation might be a pretty good use for it. He had seen it in a book little Nan had gotten from the bookmobile.

First he considered mistakes; he knew he'd done his share. Elmer remembered in particular sellin' his momma a ham last year. After a few months had gone by he had started feelin' guilty – real guilty. It was the kind of guilt that would not go away till he did something to make up for it.

"Yep," he thought, "that was a mistake." Then he thought about turning around on the heels of selling Granny the ham and giving one to Sister Alma. "Giving Alma the ham was not bad, it was just the circumstances, that was all," he mulled.

Elmer thought about how helpless he felt around Sister Alma, and how he always did exactly what she said. This scared him a little.

Whenever Elmer did voice the tiniest doubt about Sister Alma, the Virgin Birth, Immaculate Conception, or the great impregnator the Holy Ghost, it made Bert the organist as mad as a wet hen.

"Why what in the world has come over you, Elmer, talkin' like that. After all Sister Alma has done for you, and for the community. What about Uncle Joe Clemmer, and his miracle cure, and remember how she prayed over Emma's clubfoot, and made her feel better. It's like you just ain't payin' attention. I declare, Elmer, it is about to the level of blasphemy - - - BLASPHEMY." Bert was literally screaming when she finished, and Elmer had shut up right fast.

But it was just some of those "cures" that caused doubt to trickle into Elmer's mind. Everybody had heard that Uncle Joe had spent the two weeks following the "miracle cure" bedbound, and two days afterward Emma had said "seemed like her club foot really hadn't changed."

Then Elmer thought about fire, and he thought how kerosene could bring a fire back from nothing. It seemed to him like he was a dying bed of coals, that is until Alma would unleash that penetrating stare, interspersed with all those other attributes she possessed. Then it seemed like he literally roared to life, truly burning with a passion.

As Elmer reflected on this a thought hit him like an ax handle; what if sometime Sister Alma picked up the wrong can, the gas can, and lit his embers. Elmer slumped in his chair as this horrific thought sunk in. At that moment he knew he was totally helpless when it came to Sister Alma; he would do anything she asked.

It was Wednesday, 5:30pm and it was camp meeting night. Sister Alma and Polie Maxwell were sitting at the little table in the makeshift dressing room in the big tent. Polie poured two tumblers full and handed one of them to Sister Alma.

"You sure you oughta be drinkin' like this honey?" Polie asked as he watched her down the moonshine.

"Oh shut up, and pour me some more," Alma snapped. Polie Maxwell winced like he had been stabbed but dutifully poured Alma another drink. As he handed it to her he could not help but notice the change in her face over the last couple of months. About three months ago Sister Alma had possessed such a lovely complexion – that glow that many pregnant women get. But Polie noticed that the glow had faded, and now her face looked sallow and very dark circles were under her eyes. And it wasn't just looks that had changed. Polie Maxwell put the glass in front of Alma and said "Alma, I've been knowin' you a long time, and I mean knowing you – not like we just been sittin' around playin' setback. You never used to talk to me like that; what in the world has gotten into you?"

Alma stood up as quickly as her girth would allow and stalked the couple of feet until she was right in front of his honor. Her eyes were blazing like machine guns as she raised her finger, shaking it viciously in front of Polie Maxwell's nose.

"I'll tell ya what's got into me – that little gift you left off in there, unless you've dumbed down to the level of the rest of 'em and believe that the Holy Ghost came in the dead of night and screwed me. You ignorant son of a bitch. Yes Polie, that's what happened, ol' Holy Ghost rolled in here and bent me over and the party was on."

Polie Maxwell had felt the tension building in Alma for the last couple of weeks, but he was in no way prepared for this assault.

Polie turned as if to leave, and Alma grabbed his arm and pulled him back hard, almost making her fall with the effort.

"I'm not finished with your ass, hotshot. You got off so easy, just sittin' pretty while I still have two camp meetings a week; the way I am, and still workin' like a dog. And you ain't doin' shit, unless drinking beer and counting your lucky stars that I saved your sorry ass is called a job. If I hadn't come up with the Virgin Birth you would be dead meat – no political career, no daddy-in-law throwin' money to you, no friggin' nothing."

Polie's jaw started quivering and he bolted from the dressing room just ahead of the heavy glass tumbler that whistled by his head.

Alma collapsed in her chair and downed the rest of the shine. She didn't feel right, hadn't for the last day or two. "Guess it's just part of the birth deal," she said out loud. Then she again thought about the recently departed mayor, and started to get mad all over again. But she stopped herself when she realized it was almost six o'clock. Chief Usher Elmer would be by in a bit, so she needed to get dressed.

Chief Usher Elmer strode across the gravel parking lot in front of the big tent. Bert was already heading toward the organ with her music, and little Nan was playing with the other kids in the grassy area adjacent to the Holy Tent. He had been stewing a little about Sister Alma, and how she looked and had been acting. He knew how pregnant women could get out of sorts, but somehow Sister Alma's actions seemed beyond the normal. He thought about this very thing as he approached the tent, then decided to clear his mind of all of it, for he had his preparatory prayer for the Divine Child offering to think about and Sister Alma had asked him to come by a little early. If his memory had served him correctly, and he was sure it did, something a little extra was in store for ol' Elmer.

He called out "Sister Alma," as he stopped outside the curtain at the makeshift dressing room.

"Come in," she caroled, and Elmer entered. Sister Alma was in a sheer shimmering red dressing gown. The light at the mirror was behind her, and Buford could see that she had absolutely – ABSOLUTELY- nothing underneath. Elmer swallowed hard, and was eternally grateful that he did not have a dip of snuff in his mouth.

"Come see me, my precious Chief Usher Elmer," Alma called, raising her lovely arms toward him. Elmer had no control as he walked like Frankenstein toward her. When he got within a foot she grabbed him by the arms and pulled him close, and gave him a deep kiss on the lips, her tongue darting in. Second time Buford was grateful for not having a dip of snuff in his mouth.

Sister Alma released the big red-faced man and said "Sit down, Elmer, we need to talk." Elmer sat down as Alma maneuvered unsteadily to the table and brought back two tumblers filled with the Oodley Creek concoction.

"Now Elmer, I am going to call on you to assume another small duty, although it is a very important one. You have noticed, I am sure that with all of my additional weight that I am a little unsteady on my feet," Alma said, sipping the clear liquid.

Elmer looked at Sister Alma as he downed the shine in one gulp. He saw the lines around her eyes and the very dark circles beneath them; seemed like all of it had appeared over the last couple of months. Elmer thought back to the gasoline and the fire, and the mistake, and resisted his impulse to run out of the dressing room and not stop 'til he was sitting by the pot-bellied stove in his living room. Instead he said "What can I do to help Sister Alma?"

"Well Elmer," she said cupping an enormous breast and looking intently at the head usher, I want you to assist me on and off the stage, and stay up there with me at all times."

Elmer sighed with relief; her buildup had made him think it was going to be some bizarre request. This sounded pretty tame.

"Why sure, Sister Alma, I will be glad to do that. I had noticed you had been a little unsteady on your feet lately," Elmer said, while wondering if it was the extra weight, or the volume of Oodley Creek Shine and Johnny Walker Red that was causing it.

"Elmer, I will be eternally grateful to you dear. Now go about your Head Usher duties and when you get the crowd in and settled, remember to come back here and assist me onto the stage. And remember, little Nan is going to introduce me tonight. Did she practice her words, Sweet Elmer?" Alma caroled, standing up as Buford did and wrapping her arms around him.

"Ye, yes, Sister Alma, she is ready to go," Elmer stammered. Alma kissed him again, deeply, thrusting her tongue in his mouth, a long time. She finally pulled away and Elmer left the dressing room. His head was spinning, but it wasn't from the shine.

As the faithful started to arrive Elmer gathered his little band of ushers down front. There was Joe Beck Clonger, T.G. Preacher Clonger, Pasour Rhyne and a new one, Stan Guess. Stan was an easygoing farmer who lived up above Elmer's baby brother Russ. Stan had come on to fill in for "Preacher" Clonger while Preacher was serving a two-week suspension. Seems that there was some dispute about a seating arrangement; Ralph Fullbright, or "Half Bright" as they called him, had hopped into a seat that "Preacher" had prepared for Will and Hazel Carter, respected local grocers in High Shoals. When Preacher tried to persuade Half Bright to abdicate the seat, Ralph refused. Preacher picked him up and slung him down the aisle, accompanying the toss with "God damned Son of a Bitch." Preacher got his moniker honest. Half Bright whined around to Sister Alma and she told Elmer to invoke the two-week suspension. But after Preacher returned, everybody liked the congenial Stan so much that they kept him on. Of course this meant that Pasour Rhyne was not called on as much. So that was the usher core, Hoover Carpenter not showing up very often, Polie Maxwell keeping his stinky ass busy down on Oodley Creek.

Elmer looked over his group, remembering that Stan's inclusion had actually been a "godsend" as Alma would say, for Bogus Clonger had been appointed Chief Engineer, due to his skill with the lighting, and especially for his work with the spotlight. Yep, Stan worked out fine. Elmer remembered that Russ' boy Clyde tied sacks for Stan when he was doing combining work, and that Clyde always spoke highly of Stan.

Looking up Elmer saw Russ and Sarah entering the tent, and to his surprise he saw his momma shuffling in, dressed up in the black dress with the crocheted white collar – her favorite. Chief Usher Elmer reckoned that Granny had come to hear little Nan give the night's introduction of Sister Alma, but he wondered if maybe she wasn't more than a little curious about the goings on down here. He also thought that maybe it didn't hurt none that her son was the Chief Usher and her daughter-in-law Sister Alma's organist. Elmer's chest puffed out a bit as he considered this possibility.

"Hey Momma," Elmer said as he got them seated. Granny grinned her toothless grin and said "Well Elmer, I swanney if you don't look fine. And, I see Bert over there warming up. Where is that little speaker Nan; I must give her a hug."

"Oh, she'll be getting' up there on the stage in a few minutes to do her introduction. I'll see you later 'cause it is about time for me to fetch Sister Alma."

"Whaddayamean fetch Sister Alma?" asked Russ.

"Well Russ, she has gotten so large with the blessed child of the Holy Ghost that she has asked me to assist her on and off the stage, and to be up there while she is onstage, just in case she needs anything."

"Oh," said Russ, as he and the redhead exchanged curious looks.

"It's 'bout time," said Elmer. "I will see ya later."

The last of the faithful were getting to their seats as Bert the Organist started playing "Shall We Gather at the River." Perfectly on cue Chief Engineer Bogus Clonger dimmed the house lights low.

Little Nan walked up the four steps to the stage alone, and stood in the middle toward the front. When she stopped, her momma, 40A organist Bert, stopped playing and Chief Engineer Bogus hit the spotlight, which he had positioned perfectly to make a bright circle around Little Nan. There was total silence in the tent as Little Nan launched into her introduction. She had totally memorized and had recited it multiple times in front of the Rhode Island Red hens at the chicken house. Her last recitation had been interrupted by the rooster, who loved to sneak up behind her and try to spur her on the leg; however, she had been able to elude him.

She began, "All powerful and mighty Holy Ghost, mate of our own saintly Sister Alma, and father of the child of the virgin birth, the holy babe of Immaculate Conception, we pray and beseech thee to bless this gathering of the faithful and to give Sister Alma strength in these final days of her Holy Gestation.

And now, Ladies and Gentlemen, Sister Alma." As she said these last words little Nan lifted her arm, extending it toward her daddy, Chief Usher Elmer, and Sister Alma as they ascended the steps.

Bogus shifted the spotlight to Elmer and Sister Alma. Chief Usher Elmer had a stronghold on Alma; she was very unsteady on her feet. Elmer had found her passed out and had quickly patted her face down with water to bring her around.

"I wonder how much more of Oodley Creek she had after I left," Elmer considered.

Sister Alma was wearing a pure white loose-fitting gown that had tiny little pleats. She had powdered her face profusely in an attempt to hide the wrinkles and the dark circles under her bloodshot eyes. Her hair was more than a bit askew and her lipstick was a lot darker than she had worn in a long time and looked like little Nan may have applied it.

Chief Usher Elmer was aware of how disheveled she looked, but figgered that it was way too late in the game to do anything about it.

"Guess we'll see how it goes," he thought to himself as he ushered her to mid-stage.

The crowd thundered applause as the two reached Little Nan, the Bogus driven spotlight hanging on them. When they reached her, Nan gave Sister Alma a hug and curtsied to the crowd. She then skipped off the stage.

The parishioners erupted anew, clapping and shouting. There were some "Hosannas," and some "Hallelujahs," and a lot of "Praise the Lords."

As this subsided Pasour Rhyne ran up on the stage and stood beside Sister Alma, making the Larson-Savoney sign repeatedly and shouting at the top of his lungs – "Divine Intervention, Divine Intervention, Divine Intervention." Joe Beck and Preacher Clonger pulled him off the stage quickly and sat him down beside his momma and told him to shut the hell up or they would "Kick his fu—— ass." Apparently this struck a note with him and he quieted down.

Elmer stood beside Sister Alma until the din subsided. Then she said in a low voice, "Go on back to the rear of the stage, I'm okay now."

Elmer looked at her and doubted her words, but dutifully walked away and stood at the back of the stage, a good twenty feet from Sister Alma.

Total quiet now descended on the group, and Alma moved her eyes slowly from left to right, then back again. As her gaze returned to the center of the group, a beatific smile came to her face. Organist Bert began playing "Just As I Am" slowly and lowly, and perfectly on cue Chief Engineer Bogus Clonger brought up the house lights a little, doused the spotlight, then doused the house lights for five seconds. Then he hit Sister Alma with the spot. She was so ready, beaming, ready to bring the message.

She began. "Oh brothers and sisters in the community of worship in Almighty God, and the Holy Ghost – Know ye of the great divine love and adoration for the Holy Ghost, and the wonderful feeling of eternal gratitude I possess knowing that I, Sister Alma, was chosen from all the women in the world to be the receptive vessel for the immaculately conceived child of the Holy Ghost. She stopped suddenly and gave that hard stare to the audience. Then she screamed, "Can anybody say Amen, can anybody say Amen, can anybody say Hallelujah?"

The throng thundered back, louder than ever. "Amen, hallelujah, amen, hallelujah, amen," over and over and louder and louder, until Sister Alma, forgetting her condition, tried to do that little fast paced high stepping routine she used to do, circling around the front of the stage. But the weight, and the Johnny Walker Red, and the Oodley Creek shine converged in a momentous trinity and she fell flat on her ample ass. As she did what looked like a gallon of water rushed out from under her dress onto the stage.

Chief Usher Elmer rushed to her side, and B. F. House, local undertaker and ambulance service operator ran up on the stage. He called out to the colored boy he usually kept with him "Deanie, get out there and back the ambulance up to the tent, then bring in the gurney. Her water has broke and we need to get her to Garrison General Hospital as soon as possible."

"But her doctor is Fesperman in Lincolnton," Elmer protested.

"No time," cautioned the undertaker, it's five miles to Gastonia and fifteen to Lincolnton. Go call Dr. Fesperman and ask him to come over there to Garrison, you know, on Broad Street." Elmer ran out to go to the pay phone at the Sinclair station at the crossroads. When Deanie returned with the gurney he and B. F. House loaded up the passed-out Sister Alma and pushed her out the rear of the tent to the waiting white ambulance. Chief Engineer Bogus kept the spotlight on the gurney 'til it passed outside the tent.

The crowd appeared to be in shock. Their leader was gone; a power vacuum. Then striding up to the stage steps came two tall women. It was Winnie and Mary Froneberger, spinster sisters who taught at Costner Elementary School. These two women were not just solid community leaders, they were Rocks; in fact, they had taught many of the younger ones in the throng. Miss Winnie was the more dominant of the two, so she walked up on the stage and immediately went over to Organist Bert and spoke a few sentences to her. Bert, who had been weeping, wiped her tears, nodded in agreement, smiled, and stood up and walked off the stage. Miss Winnie sat down behind the organ and looked out at the confused bunch.

Without saying a word Miss Winnie launched into "The Yellow Rose of Texas." She banged hard on the organ keys, just the way she hit the piano keys on the old upright on the stage at Costner School. She had a big, wide infectious smile, and you could always see the small tarnish on one of her front teeth where the porcelain had worn a little on the cap.

"She's the sweetest little rosebud, that Texas ever knew, her eyes they are like diamonds, they sparkle like the dew, you can talk about your Clementine, and sing of Rosa Lee, but the Yellow Rose of Texas is the only gal for me," she caroled.

Once she came to the end of the song she just started over. She was bellowing out the words, and her sister Miss Mary was standing at the front of the stage; Miss Mary started exhorting the crowd to join in the singing, starting to pump her arms up and down like the bandleader Mitch Miller and flashing that big Thornburg smile.

About halfway through the second round of "Yellow Rose of Texas" the crowd was on their feet, singing boisterously. Even Chief Usher Elmer who would be taxed to carry a tune in a tin tub, was giving it his best.

After the second go round of the song Miss Winnie stopped on the organ, and at Miss Winnie's urging Chief Engineer Bogus dropped the house lights and hit the Spotlight on Miss Mary Froneberger who stood stock-still at center stage displaying a mournful countenance.

Everybody around Dallas went to Costner Elementary School, so when they saw that look on Miss Mary's face they knew what was coming, and as one they jumped to their feet cheering.

Costner Elementary School was the typical red brick school built in the WPA era – classrooms radiating around the central auditorium. Once a week there would be Assembly, led by Miss Winnie, who was the principal. She would bang on the old upright piano and lead the singing, and The Yellow Rose of Texas was one of her favorites. After that Miss Mary would tell the story of "Cousin Orley," and that is what had the crowd in a tizzy of delightful recollection.

She began, maintaining her mournful countenance. "When I was a little girl, I had a first cousin who lived next door to me. His name was Orley. I liked Orley a lot, and he liked me too!" When Miss Mary said this she dropped her face a little and then looked upward, shyly. It worked well; she captured the little girl look.

"Well Orley was a real good boy," she said, "and he did well in school and went to church and was just about perfect 'cept for one thing." As one the throng shouted out "and what was that Miss Mary?"

Miss Mary did not miss a beat. "Well I'm glad you asked," and she offered a little girl smile.

"As I said, he was might near perfect but for one fault; he liked to play up around the railroad tracks behind our house up on the ridge. No matter how much his momma told him not to, he would wind up playin' on those tracks. Well one day 'bout suppertime Orley's momma started callin' for him, over and over, but Orley wouldn't answer and was nowhere to be seen. Finally she came over to our house and asked me if I would go up and try to find Orley, 'cause she was cookin' rice and feared she might scorch it. So knowin' Orley well, I figgered I would go up the ridge to the train track, 'cause that's where he more than likely was."

The audience was fixed on her every word – spellbound, as transfixed to her as the yellow circle of light was to Miss Mary.

Little Lois was listening with rapt attention, as was Sarah, for Miss Mary had taught Sarah in the first grade also, and the story was alive even back then.

"As I got about halfway up the ridge, I heard the six o'clock train blow its whistle, and felt the vibration in the forest floor as it passed by," Miss Mary said. "And when I got up to the tracks there was Orley, (a long pause) and over there was Orley, (a long pause) and then way over yonder was Orley." Miss Mary pointed dramatically in a different direction as she described the locations of the late Orley.

Such a thunder of applause and laughter erupted as she stood there, bowing deeply and beaming that big Froneberger smile.

"Thank you and good night," Miss Mary said, and she and Miss Winnie walked quietly off the stage.

Russ, Sarah and Little Lois were still laughing, and Granny was commenting on "what a fine tale spinner that Mary is, reminds me of my late husband John David."

They walked to the car and on the ride home Granny wondered, "How ya reckon that Sister Alma might be, Russ?"

Russ thought for a moment as he motored them down 321 North toward Clonger Dairy Road. "I don't know, Granny, there's been a lot of rumors about Sister Alma lately, talk of her drinking a lot. I don't know, but I swear, she looked drunk tonight," he said.

"Well I'll Swanney," sighed Granny.

"I think maybe she is to be pitied," added Sarah as they drove past the silos of the dairy and turned onto the washboard red dirt road.

Two days had passed, and Sister Alma was lying in bed on the third floor of Garrison General Hospital on S. Broad Street in Gastonia, N.C. Alma was loosely holding a one and a half day infant girl in her chubby right arm, sort of cradling the baby up against her right side.

Dr. Fesperman was at her bedside. Alma looked at the skinny little girl and watched her; she twitched and shivered, twitched and shivered. "What did you say they called it?" she inquired of the good doctor.

"Fetal Alcohol Syndrome," replied Dr. Fesperman, giving Sister Alma a wry look. "Maybe you remember my warnings about Johnny Walker and Mr. Oodley?" he said.

"Aw, hush with the sermon; thought you were a doctor, not a preacher. If I want to get chastised that way I'll go confess to Preacher Krummitt up at Lander's Chapel," she said. "Can't you give her a shot, or something, and straighten her little ass out?" Alma implored.

Dr. Fesperman shook his head and looked dead on at the evangelist. "Alma, I will be totally straight up with you; there ain't a shot in this world that can help this child, and I'll tell you the bottom line – I have never seen one of these babies last much longer than a day or two."

Sister Alma looked at him blankly; no, actually looked right through the doctor as if he weren't there.

"Okay," she said, emotionless, "Thank you Doctor." Dr. Fesperman turned and went out the door. Sister Alma was alone in the room, and she started thinking, thinking about maybe the biggest religious bash ever seen in Dallas. Alma thought in the quiet, very loosely holding the twitching child, until she had it set in her mind.

"It will be fantastic," she said out loud, and reached back and grabbed one of the pillows under her head and gently, very gently, placed it over the face of the child that she had named Virginia Mary, placed it gently, but very, very firmly, until the child stopped twitching, and then for good measure held the pillow there another five minutes. Then Sister Alma replaced the pillow behind her head and took a nap.

Word spread quickly the next day about the tragic death of the Holy Child Virginia Mary. Of course everyone was very sad about the loss, but they were heartened and encouraged by Alma's quick recovery. Word was she was already home and doing just fine. Sister Alma had said that the Child had been born with the "shakin' palsy," and that apparently her little system, as holy as it was, was not able to overcome this tremendous disadvantage.

The parishioners seemed to be comfortable with this sad explanation, and Dr. Fesperman left well enough alone and had no comment.

Sister Alma put out the word through her parishioners and the local paper, the Gastonia Gazette, that the viewing would be on Saturday evening at Dallas Funeral Home, with the funeral service on Sunday afternoon at Puett's Chapel United Methodist Church on the Dallas-Cherryville Highway. The location was a no brainer for Alma; it was where Chief Usher Elmer and Organist Bert belonged and attended every Sunday.

Sister Alma had met with B. F. House, owner of the Dallas Funeral Home the day before the viewing to get the logistics and the finances straight. She came to his office on the bottom floor of the Dallas Funeral Home, back in the rear left corner.

B. F. House greeted her and asked her to sit down; he was resplendent in a black suit and starched white shirt and a modest tie – he had overseen a funeral that afternoon.

"B. F., I need to cut to the chase, I have no money but I can pay you after the viewing, for I know there will be a huge love offering and whatever it is will be yours," Alma said.

B. F. House looked at Alma with his most caring look, the one he saved for his most valued customers and said, "Sister Alma," his brilliantly white smile beaming, (for he had brand new very expensive false choppers), "you can be at ease at this point. All of the arrangements, including the ambulance ride to Garrison General, have been taken care of – you are not to concern yourself with these mundane things in your time of grief."

For once in her life Sister Alma was totally flummoxed; she could not believe her ears; moreover, she could not comprehend her good fortune.

Sister Alma stared at B. F. and tried to say "Wh – wh – wh," but before she could complete the question the door opened and in strode a beaming Polie Maxwell. Alma was overcome with emotion, and rose to meet the Honorable Mayor and share a lengthy embrace. B. F. House, always the polished and savvy gentleman, quietly departed, leaving the two of them in the office.

Sister Alma was sitting quietly, thinking and plotting. Her plan was going to require very careful planning and coordination, but she thought she had all the bases covered. Polie Maxwell's family had a long-abandoned graveyard way out in the country near Lucia. B. F. House was on board; he didn't care, as long as he got paid. And Alma knew enough about the undertaker to know that he could keep his mouth shut.

The viewing was at 8 p.m. and it was five already. Alma hurried over to the Dallas Funeral Home to meet local photographer Johnny Kamp. She had already seen him once today, this morning when he had taken several shots of Virginia Mary in her little pink coffin. Now they were meeting so Alma could collect the 8 x 10 photos. Johnny Kamp was waiting inside the funeral home when she got there.

"Here they are Alma, 500 of them, glossy finish. So my deal is a quarter apiece after you sell them right?"

Alma grabbed the 8 x 10's and looked them over. They were good quality; Johnny did all the work for the Dallas High School annual. He had picked the right one to reproduce, the most angelic one, and true to Alma's directions had spot shaded around Virginia Mary's little head to make a hint of a halo.

Alma was satisfied. "Now Johnny, you know I can pay you tomorrow; these things will all be gone tonight, she said.

"No problem" said Johnny. "On the morrow," he said and went out the door.

Alma walked back to her house. She had to get dressed, and she had to be back at the Dallas Funeral Home at 6:30 to coordinate the next step.

Chief Usher Elmer was dressed in his best suit, and he was checkin' himself out in the long mirror, and holdin' his stomach in.

"Looks alright," he said out loud, and went into the living room where Bert and Little Nan were waiting. Bert was in a loose black dress and Naomi was in her play clothes. They were gonna drop Nan off at Russ and Sarah's, the idea being that a wake would be a bit much for the little girl; additionally, Russ and Sarah were not going to the viewing – something about having a lot of things to catch up on.

The three trooped outside and got in the car for the short ride to the old house. Granny, Russ, Sarah and Little Lois were sitting on the front porch when they pulled up. The three of them got out and walked up on the pine-floored porch.

They all exchanged hellos, then Elmer said, "Russ, you sure you and Sarah don't want to come down to little Virginia Mary's wake; it would be a nice way to convey your sorrow." Elmer thought a second about "convey," his new word. Alma had taught it to him and this was the first chance he had had to use it.

"I guess not Elmer" said Russ, his lower lip bulging with a load of snuff. "We just got a lot of things to do; anyway, it will give Lois and Nan a chance to play." The two girls had already run into the side yard and were halfway up the big China Berry tree.

"Well, you give our heartfelt regards to Sister Alma," said Granny. Elmer and Bert said they would and left. They got in the car and headed to Dallas. They were going to be early but there was a reason; Sister Alma had asked them to stand beside her in the receiving line. They were very honored and proud.

Chief Engineer Bogus Clonger had enlisted Pasour Rhyne to help him move the big spotlight to the Dallas Funeral Home. After much grunting and cussing they finally got the awkward contraption loaded into the back of Bogus' blue pickup truck. Well, it was mostly blue; the driver's side door had a brown exterior due to Bogus' backer spittin' out the window. Sister Alma had told the Chief Engineer exactly where to set up the light in the long parlor – the largest room in the funeral home. The spotlight would be all the way at one end and would be directed on the end of the little pink coffin, the end where her angelic head lay. Bogus and Pasour fumbled around and got it set up, then practiced turning it on and off, making sure it was focused exactly on the right spot. Sister Alma had given specific instructions about this; when the crowd had gathered in the room funeral director House would walk over and open the little pink coffin which housed the sanctified daughter of the union of the Holy Ghost and Sister Alma.

Bogus, satisfied he had everything under control, told Pasour Rhyne to return to the room a little before eight.

Pasour wandered out the back door and stood looking over at the FCX Store that backed up to the funeral home. Pasour was very proud of himself; he had been able to hide his fury very well.

"Them two sons o' bitches that jerked me off the stage, they'll get it and get it good," he thought to himself, "but I'll deal with them later. That Bitch Alma had 'em do it; ain't nobody gonna embarrass me like that never, ever again."

Pasour grinned his crazy grin and thought about his first plan, the one he had shit-canned. He had planned to wait until about eight o'clock, when the crowd would be the biggest, and then pile up the bales of FCX pine straw against the side of the funeral home then the gas, then the match, and what a show it would be. But Pasour had decided that it would not be fair to Blair Falls to burn up his business, so he went to Plan B. Pasour

Rhyne grinned his crazy ass gin, gave the Larson Savoney sign to the empty yard, and wandered down Trade Street to Lewis Sumney's Drugstore; he had an hour to kill.

The eight o'clock hour was nearing as the throng gathered in the big parlor, spilling out into all the other rooms and even onto the wrap-around porch.

Sister Alma was standing by the little pink coffin with Chief Usher Elmer and Organist Bert by her side. Elmer had his hat off and had adopted an appropriately somber expression. Organist Bert was dewy-eyed. Sister Alma's face was expressionless, but her mind was going a mile a minute, counting up her cut from the pictures – they would clamber to get them once the coffin was opened. Then Alma thought about the new crusades, and how she might be nationally famous once this story hit the papers.

Finally the moment arrived and B. F. shot a glance at Sister Alma. Then Blair motioned toward Chief Engineer Bogus. The lights had been lowered, and as B. F. House lifted the lid of the little pink coffin the brilliant spear of the spotlight focused inside the empty coffin.

The crowd gasped as one. Sister Alma looked into the little pink coffin and turned to the parishioners. "She has ascended into Heaven," she shouted.

Pasour Rhyne had worked his way through the crowd all the way up to the coffin. He had his hand on the .32 pistol in his pocket and as Alma finished her exclamation Pasour moved to within three feet of the earthly mother of the sanctified child of the Holy Ghost, shouted "You God damned Bitch," and pumped a bullet into her forehead. Sister Alma fell straight backwards, and as the little pink coffin was on a short table she landed in the coffin sideways, her legs spread unceremoniously up in the air.

Chief Usher Elmer grabbed Pasour Rhyne and disarmed him. Pasour did not struggle, just flashed his goofy grin. In a few moments the police came and took Pasour Rhyne away. Pasour had only one regret as he was led away. The handcuffs kept him from making the Larson Savoney sign.

EPILOGUE

Pasour Rhyne walked through the dayroom, saying hello to everyone, and flashing the Larson Savoney sign to one and all. About half of them returned the sign, crossing the right arm across the forehead, the left arm across the waist, and wiggling the fingers of the right hand. Pasour swelled with pride when a comrade returned the sign. "It took a while for some of them to come around, but they are starting to understand," he thought. Pasour wasn't quite sure what it was he was trying to get them to understand, and for a very good reason; he didn't understand himself. Every time he tried to sort out just what Larson Savoney stood for he got all confused; he knew it had something to do with meetings down on the South Fork River, that fire played a part, and that doing the sign was important. "You know," he said out loud, "just ain't gonna worry about it – it will all be revealed later."

Pasour Rhyne hummed "Farther Along We'll Know More About It' as he found a chair in the dayroom and opened the letter from his mother. It was addressed to:

Pasour Rhyne
Western Carolina Center for the Criminally Insane
Morganton, N.C. 28034

Pasour began to read: "Dear Son, I hope you are feeling okay and that they are feeding you good. Things have kind of settled down around here since the judge ruled that you was non compos mentis. Some tent company came and took away the tent – seems Sister Alma was making payments on it. Rumor has it that Paul Ramseur from Stanley might get a good price on the repossessed tent.

Pasour, I just want you to know that we love you no matter what you done, and hope that some day you can return home.

Love Momma"

Pasour rubbed the side of his head at the temple, rubbed the baseball sized shaved spot on each side of his head.

This sounded quite curious to Pasour because he did not remember doing anything.

"Oh well," he considered, "Momma is getting' on up in age, and a mite forgetful." This thought somehow made him feel considerable better. Then came another thought. "Seems that's the way it works, thoughts coming back a little at a time." But this one made Pasour Rhyne stand up straight, and with a big smile on his face he shouted "DIVINE INTERVENTION."

THE PROPHET EZEKIEL

Part 1—THE CALLING

Zeke Taylor was in the hole. It was not actually a hole, but prison lingo for solitary confinement. That was the bad news; the good news was that he had only three days left there, and the even better news was that when he returned to the regular prison population at the Ranlo Prison Facility he was set to be released in another ten days. Solitary had not been so awful bad; Zeke had been there a couple of times before while he was serving out his DUI and probation violation conviction. "Runnin' my mouth while I was all coked up didn't help much," he said out loud; of course it didn't matter 'cause there was no one to hear him—-the guard showed up like clockwork every hour and he had been by only ten minutes before. Zeke thought back to 9 months before, and the fateful night that set his prison stay in motion. He had been out with his buddies over at the Office Tavern and a "shipment" had come in. One could always tell when coke came into town——-all of a sudden the bar would get real busy and there would more "passes" around than in an NFL football game. Before you knew it both the men's and women's bathrooms would be packed with hungry, yearning noses, and as the say at Communion, "as these leave may others come to the table to take their places," and of course they did.

    It was after one of those manic marathon nights that Zeke Taylor found himself flying down Franklin Boulevard, going 85 by the speedometer but he was more like 2000 feet in altitude. He had been laughing like hell and singing along to "Freebird" when the blue and white Gastonia police car pulled him over. Feelin' pretty frisky he had jumped out of the car and shouted "I am an F.B.I. agent."

This salutation earned him a quick set of bracelets behind his back and the following question; "May we search your vehicle?" Zeke was way beyond caring what he said; he just wanted to be funny. "Sure fellas," he said grinning, "and while you're in there see if you can find that lighter of mine that's been missing for two weeks." Zeke thought this line was so good that he started laughing so hard that he fell up against the officer who had a hold of him. This gaiety was rewarded with a knee to the groin which sent him to the pavement to reflect on how happy he should be given his situation. After the officer who searched the car brought over a half ounce of pot and a well used little glass pipe Zeke had bought at the Kwik Mart Zeke quieted down considerably, listening to the droning recitation of "you have a right to contact an attorney" etc.

Things only got worse when they got downtown and he blew a .20 on the breathalyzer——cocaine always making him extremely thirsty. So when they were reciting the charges of speeding, reckless driving, D.U.I., criminal possession of marijuana and paraphernalia, and last but not least violation of probation from a domestic violence conviction six months previous, Zeke was feelin' pretty low. Plus, by the time he got in a cell the coke high was greatly diminished and he became one depressed little pup.

Three months and two postponements later Zeke was "processing in" to the Ranlo Minimum Security Detention Center, in preparation of serving a six months sentence. Zeke knew it could have been a lot worse; Ranlo was close to home, and he could have been sent down east to Caledonia, a prison that housed a big farm where the inmates had to work. At Ranlo you had to work only four hours a day and had all day Sunday off. But of course Zeke was in trouble quickly and got to spend his first stint in "solitary" for fighting.

Zeke Taylor was making a concerted effort to not dwell on his present situation but to ponder on how he came to be in Ranlo Prison. Whenever Zeke got into these "ponderin" modes he invariably thought of several particular occurrences at High Shoals High School, where Zeke had experienced a rather brief but very tumultuous two years. He remembered Mr. Penley, the History teacher, who personified the word "thin"————he was thin in stature, had thinning hair, and liver colored thin lips. But Mr. Penley was pretty bright and loved to use big words. Zeke Taylor recalled one time when he got caught throwing spitballs and his punishment was to write one hundred times "I must not hurl projectiles with prolific velocity." On another occasion Mr. Penley was going on about Egyptian ruins and introduced the class to the word "scatology" and of course its meaning. Each year when Ned Penley got to this chapter he braced himself for all the giggles and titters that would ensue. When the din finally died down Zeke had raised his hand. After being recognized by Mr. Penley Zeke had stood up and in his best George Stevens "Kingfish" impersonation rolled his eyes around and said "Well sir, I believes I done deee-cided what I wants to do wif my life—-I wants to be one of dem scatologists, cause then you can get into everybody's shit." Everyone in the class, with the noted absence of Mr. Ned Penley, heehawed. The less than impressed Mr. Costner promptly ushered Zeke Taylor to Principal Eldridge's office and after reciting the problem left Zeke with the towering principal. Principal Charles Eldridge was 6' 2" tall and weighed every bit of 350 pounds. He wore a starched white shirt everyday and wheezed when he talked. The cause of his labored breathing was nestled in each of the front pockets of his shirt——he kept a pack of Winston cigarettes in each one all the time.

"Well son, I guess you know what is coming to you," Principal Eldridge said, stopping for a few moments for a coughing fit. Then he lit another Winston from the one smoldering in his giant overflowing ashtray and reached under his desk to pull out a large wooden paddle with holes drilled in it. "Assume the position" he said, Zeke quickly bending over, this not being his first rodeo.

As the guard came and casually looked in at the brooding Zeke Taylor Zeke recollected another trip to Principal Eldridge's office, this time for telling the truth. Zeke Taylor was a firm believer in telling the truth—— when he felt like it or it was to his advantage. The particular instance he was thinking about was in Edwina Cuntress' English Class. Her real name was Edwina Countliss but Zeke had bestowed upon her the new moniker, always saying it very fast, leaving her with a bit of a confused look on her face like "did I really hear that?" Miss Countliss never openly questioned Zeke about this, correctly figgering that there was no way to win.

Mrs. Countliss was a woman in her mid fifties sporting dyed red hair, a "Blanche Dubois" accent that Zeke thought affected, and very glassy eyes furnished by her prescription "nerve pills." The rumor was that she had a philandering insurance salesman husband who drove her crazy. Mrs. Countliss also had a seven year old adopted son whom she doted on, ad nauseum. In class it was always "Frankie did this" and "Frankie did that"; Zeke got real tired of hearing 'bout Frankie real quick. The final straw that sent Zeke Taylor to a return engagement with his chain smoking principal had happened on a winter morning, on Valentine's Day. "Miss Cuntress" got off on a tangent about St. Valentine's day and how her son Frankie loved her so much. "Yes class, and I'll tell you what my sweet little man did for me this morning——-he got up early and fixed his momma breakfast." This announcement elicited the typical "awwwsssss" from the cadre of Miss Countliss' pet girl students sitting up at the front of the class, her girls beaming at her adoringly as she continued. Meanwhile Zeke was entertaining his friends by rolling his eyes and sticking his finger down his throat in disgust.

"But the most wonderful thing girls, er class, was what he did with the sausage—-he fashioned the sausage pattie into the shape of a heart." At this point Mrs. Countliss became overcome with emotion and fumbled in her purse for a tissue, three of her pet girls running to her side. Zeke Taylor, at the point of wretching called out "where was the old man this morning, bangin' his secretary?" Zeke's followers loved this comment and laughed raucously. Edwina Countliss stood bolt upright, or at least as erect as a woman having ingested five fifty milligram Darvon could. "Who said that?" she shouted and was quickly supplied with the name "Zeke Taylor" by one of her girls.

"Zeke Taylor," Mrs. Countliss shrieked, "don't you have any respect for me?"

"No, I do not Mrs. Cuntlisss" Zeke said, once again saying her name very quickly. She cocked her head a bit when she heard her name pronounced but quickly moved on. "Come with me to Mr. Eldridge's office" she screamed, and before the adoring eyes of his gang of followers in the rear of the class Zeke Taylor followed Mrs. Countliss to the Principal's office. The English teacher barged past the secretary and burst into Principal Eldridge's smoky office. She quickly blurted out what had transpired, turned on her heel, and threw back over her shoulder "I will not have a student in my class who does not respect me," and slammed the door. Charles Eldridge lifted his tired watery eyes toward Zeke and said "What in the hell did you say that for?"

"Because it's the truth; you don't want me to lie do you?" Zeke said, using his best sensitive , innocent, bewildered look. "Bend over," said Charles Eldridge, and that was Zeke Taylor's last day in English class.

But these episodes did not spell the end of Zeke Taylor's high school career; it was chronic truancy. Zeke just hated school but couldn't control himself to stay in until he was sixteen, so he just quit coming and started working with Carroll Hoffman's fence company. He loved the hard work, digging holes for the chain link fences and stretching the wire. But the truant officer did not admire Zeke's work nearly as much, so after several sessions with his parents, and an equal number of "official warnings", the powers that be deemed Zeke to be sent to Jackson Training School for 6 months. Jackson Training School was an assemblage of two story brick buildings just northeast of Charlotte whose state charter used the phrase "for the rehabilitation of wayward youth." Zeke didn't much care when he was told where he was going; his only regret was losing his job, but that fear was assuaged by his boss Carroll Hoffman's words———-"your job will be here when you get back Zeke." .Zeke felt a lot better after hearing this promise, and actually started thinking about the stint as a six month vacation, a new adventure. Plus one of his buddies, Satch Smith, was back in there now so it wouldn't be like he didn't know anybody. Satch had been in and out for years; he absolutely hated any kind of authority.

Zeke did his "time" and when he got out went back with Carroll Hoffman, and that was where he was working when he had his trouble and wound up in the Ranlo Prison.

Zeke jolted awake at the sound of the guard's hourly footsteps and went back to his pondering. He knew that he had to come up with a new idea, a new direction, or he would wind up back here in the same place or worse. Then he thought about his pal Satch Smith that he had "done time" with at Jackson Training School and shivered at the idea he may wind up where Satch was——Central Prison in Raleigh.

Zeke remembered Satch telling about the event that had sent him to his longest trip away from home ever, being convicted of attempted murder. Satch had told him the story while they were in Jackson Training School, before the authorities had concluded that the Jackson detainee had bigger fish to fry or be fried with and had charged him.

Satch had been in one of the beer joints across the Catawba River in Mecklenburg County. Satch was at "Beatty's no. 3", a one story brick building that had the old forties classic extended roof over the front where the gas pumps were. The Beatty Brothers had five of these gas station beer joints around, this one being run by a Beatty brother who had a missing hand, rumor being it was from an electrical accident. What happened was Satch and some linthead from the Ragan Cotton Mill had been playing pool, and the linthead accused Satch of cheating. An argument ensued and a fight and it moved out the back door of the bar to the gravel parking lot. "That son of a bitch was huge," Satch had told Zeke, "and he was whippin' me purty good and I was plenty worried so I pulled out my hawkbill knife, and I had it razor sharp. I gave him three swipes and he just kept coming," Satch had told him. "That's when I pulled out that little .22 from my back pocket and shot him twice."

At this juncture in the telling of the tale Satch Smith paused for a few moments. "And that's when I vowed to never carry a sharp knife again; if it hada been rusty that fucker woulda felt it and stopped, but that knife bein' so sharp I am satisfied he didn't feel shit, and that's why he just kept comin' and why I had to shoot his linthead ass," Satch had said.

Fortunately for Satch the linthead had survived, but on the other side of the coin Satch's long record combined with cutting and shooting earned him six years in the Raleigh accommodations.

Zeke Taylor shuddered in his solitary cell when he thought about Satch's fate; he knew damn well he didn't want to go that route, but the as yet undiscovered key to avoid it was what he was desperately searching for. These thoughts dominated Zeke's mind for his remaining time in solitary and continued to be with him until he was released.

Zeke Taylor's long time girlfriend Cinnamon Boylan was waiting outside the front gate when Zeke was released. Zeke was now 20 years old and Cinnamon had just turned 18, being a most recent graduate of High Shoals High School. Cinnamon was a honey blonde with pale blue eyes, tumescent lips, and a killer figure, topped off with a very ample bosom. They had been a pair for four years——four idyllic years, 'cept for when Zeke Taylor had to keep her in line. Zeke did not have to administer punishment much 'cause Cinnamon was a quick study; in fact, one black eye when she was sixteen had convinced her—-Cinnamon was IN LOVE. Zeke Taylor had got a virgin.

Cinnamon was wearing what Zeke had asked for the last time they had talked—-push up bra, skimpy blouse with tons of cleavage, short shorts, no panties. Zeke Taylor exhibited remarkable reserve, allowing Cinnamon to get about fifty yards from the main gate before he told her to pull over in front of the deserted baseball field and they jumped into the back seat and screwed like the most horny maniacs in Gaston County, for that is about what they were. Six months is a long time.

After they got clothed and on the road Zeke Taylor told Cinnamon Boylan his new game plan, in fact the only real game plan he had ever had. It had come to him only last evening and Cinnamon's eyes lit up as Zeke recounted his revelation. He filled Cinnamon in as they went down into the edge of South Carolina to the "Meadowbrook Supper Club". The "Meadowbrook" had been the scene of their first date four years before; they had burgers and beers. Of course they had been under the legal drinking age of 18, being 16 and 14 respectively, but the owners of the Meadowbrook never carded anybody. "Brian and Lucille" were an affable couple in their late fifties who always seemed drunk, at least when the High Shoals High kids were there; they served anybody and had the best cheeseburgers around. Clyde Hall's little brother walked in when he was only twelve and bought a Country Club Malt Liquor, no questions asked.

By the time the couple had arrived at the bar, ordered two long neck PBRs and two cheeseburgers Zeke had divulged the entire plan to Cinnamon. He had told her about how he could turn his life around, and how it had all come down to one question he had asked himself that last night in prison—

———"at what point in my life did I feel the most 'alive' and productive, like I was doing something I was really good at, talented at."

Cinnamon was listening intently; she truly worshipped Zeke Taylor and always hung on every word he said. "What was it Zeke, what did you come up with?" Cinnamon asked, draining the last of her PBR. Zeke's eyes got brighter as he recounted his "defining moment" to his woman.

"You member a coupla years ago when sister Alma had her tent up around Boger City, and how Roger Haas had gone up there and pretended to be crazy and talked gibberish in front of the crowd, and how Sister Alma 'cured' him in front of everybody?" Zeke asked. Cinnamon nodded and said "and he took you up there didn't he?" "El correcto," Zeke said, "and I met her before the service and showed her my spastic walk thing I do so well and she hired me on the spot to appear before her believers. And I did my crazy act and she 'cured' me in front of everybody. I swear, that was the most fun I ever had in my life. Well I started thinkin' 'bout that the other night and I also started thinking about how much fun sister Alma seemed to be having; then it came to me why everything that day was so cool, so good————here is a woman who has got everybody fooled, everybody conned, is having the time of her life and is making a ton of money while she does it."

Zeke's voice had gotten louder as he was recounting his experience to Cinnamon, to the point where he was almost shouting. Brian, the bar owner, even came over to check on him, lurching toward Zeke as he clumsily maneuvered his drunken ass behind the bar. "You alright Zeke?" Brian asked. Being assured by Zeke that everything was okay the proprietor fixed himself a quick drink and stumbled away.

As Brian departed Zeke got back to the affair at hand. "I knew right then that was my calling, and I knew damn well that if I could get my shit straight I could make it work, and that is exactly what I plan on doing," Zeke said, looking excitedly at Cinnamon Boylan. Cinnamon was excited also. "Well how ya gonna pull it off Zeke?" she asked, pursing her pretty lips and staring at Zeke with her gorgeous eyes.

"Well I gotta think about that whole thing a little bit, 'cause I know I can do it but I wish I had somebody to guide me a little, and of course Sister Alma is dead, shot in the forehead by that idiot Pasour Rhyne. And it sure wouldn't do a damn bit of good to talk to Pasour Rhyne, 'cause although he was around Sister Alma and the oranization for several years I wouldn't believe anything he said," said Zeke.

A long silence followed Zeke's statement and then his eyes got lit up again. "Sister Alma's boyfriend, the mayor, Polie Maxwell is still around ain't he baby?" Zeke asked Cinnamon. Cinnamon told him that Polie Maxwell was indeed 'still around', but his stature in the town had been considerably diminished by the negative publicity after Sister Alma had been killed. He had indeed fallen on hard times, been voted out of office and was also a victim of failing health. All of these issues combined with some severe business reversals had landed Polie Maxwell in the "County Home", a facility for the impoverished and destitute elderly.

"My daddy goes over to see him every week, and I can get him to see if Polie Maxwell would be willing for us to come see him," Cinnamon said, getting excited about the possibility of her being able to offer some help in Zeke's ambitious idea. "Baby, that would be fantastic; talk to your daddy and let me know when we go see him," Zeke said. As they drank another long neck PBR, or "blue in a bottle" as they called it their conversation turned to other things, but when Cinnamon dropped Zeke Taylor off at his parents' house where he lived in a little garage apartment, they agreed that she would call him the next morning after she had talked with her father, hopefully with some good news about the prospective visit to the County Home to see Polie Maxwell.

True to her word Cinnamon called Zeke at ten o'clock the next morning, assuring him that she had the "full story" on Polie Maxwell and she would share it with him as they rode over to the "County Home".

Zeke hopped into the car and listened intently as Cinnamon Boylan told what she had learned about the besmirched mayor. "Well Zeke, you know Polie Maxwell and my daddy have always been buddies, so if anybody knows everything about Polie it is him. Like we were talking about yesterday it is no secret that Polie Maxwell has fallen on rough times, and it goes beyond reputation and finances. Daddy told me that even though Polie is only seventy years old he has severe dementia; daddy said it is very odd, 'cause he can be very clear thinking one minute and not even know his name the next. Plus he will go off on these long ramblings about things that don't make a lot of sense. Daddy says that Polie Maxwell has always been real smart, and at one time wanted to be a comedy writer. Guess that might explain some of his mental meanderings," Cinnamon concluded. Zeke took it all in. "But we can ask him about Sister Alma, right?" Zeke asked. "Of course", said Cinnamon, "Daddy goes to see Polie every week and he says he is always talkin' 'bout her".

"I remember Polie Maxwell quite well, and I think he may remember me, am purty sure he was up at Boger City at the tent when I made my 'debut'. I also remember that he loved a drink. Let's take a lil detour; turn down Cloninger Road and take that first right", said Zeke' When they got down to the end of the dirt road Zeke got out and knocked on the door of the tiny tin roofed shack in the clearing. A short grimy man came out on the front porch pulling a game left leg along with him. "Hey Baxter," said a grinning Zeke Taylor, "ain't this a hell of a note." The two of them talked congenially, Zeke asking about Baxter's leg. "Cut it with a saw, that's why I do upholstery work now, and of course help ol' Joe Keener out a little," he grinned slyly. Zeke told Baxter he was goin' to see Polie Maxwell and that he needed a quart of shine. Baxter walked back inside and immediately returned with a jar in a paper sack. "Still five dollars?" Zeke asked, digging for his wallet. "This one's on me," said Baxter as he handed Zeke the goods. "Some of Oodley Creek's finest; made it myself. And tell the Mayor hello for me. Let's have a drink," Baxter said, unscrewing the lid of the mason jar and taking a healthy gulp, then handing it to Zeke who followed suit. Zeke then secured the jar, said goodbye to Baxter, and hopped in beside Cinnamon. Zeke offered his woman a drink, which she quickly took and grinned at her as he said "now on to the County Home, and the secrets of the late sister Alma."

Part 2—THE ANOINTMENT

Zeke and Cinnamon drove back to the Dallas Crossroads and took a right on the Cherryville highway. Only a half mile on the left was a road that meandered for 200 yards to an old nineteenth century columned two story house——-the "County Home". They parked in the rutted gravel driveway and walked up the three steps to a wide veranda and entered the building. It was sunny outside so when they walked in it took a while for their eyes to adjust; the two of them just stood inside the door for a minute. As their eyes came around they saw a reception desk about twenty feet inside; seated behind the desk was a lady of about 65 with dyed orange hair dressed in a white uniform with a name tag pinned on her chest proclaiming her to be Vergie Propst, R.N. She looked up and said "May I help you?" The foyer they were in was large, about twenty feet square. The desk was situated in a corner, with tall double French doors flanking it. Zeke and Cinnamon could hear low murmurings in the background behind the doors. A stairway to the left of the desk had been permanently blocked off.

Cinnamon spoke up as they approached the desk, "Yes ma'am, we are here to see Polie Maxwell, he is a good friend of my father's," Cinnamon said, smiling her sweetest smile, then pursing her pretty lips. "Oh yes", said Vergie Propst R. N.,"just follow me". They went behind the stodgy nurse, Zeke being careful to kind of keep the paper sack of shine down low by his leg as Miss Propst had perused them briefly before heading to the French doors. But before she reached the doors Vergie Propst stopped suddenly and walked back to her desk, returning with a 12 ounce cup.

"Young man, fill up this cup and we'll be okay," Nurse Propst said, grinning at a wide eyed Zeke Taylor. Zeke was born on a day, but "it wuddn't yesterday". Zeke filled her up and Vergie Propst sipped on the elixir as she opened the door and led them inside. As they worked their way along the visitors saw that this bottom floor was divided into three large rooms; there was no hall, so you had to walk through one room to get to another.

About every ten feet 2x4s had been installed, being attached to the floor and the ceiling, and clothes line wire had been tied to hooks that had been screwed into the lumber. The curious construction provided cubicles of approximately ten feet by ten feet, a modicum of privacy being achieved by assorted blankets and bedspreads being hung on the wires. A single light bulb hanging from the ceiling provided each cubicle with 60 watts of illumination.

As Zeke and Cinnamon walked behind Miss Propst they noticed the rancor of dead air and feces, not overpowering, but still very much there. They could not see in most of the areas, but a few had a blanket pulled open a bit, and some of the inhabitants were sitting on the side of their cot and others lying down. "Not so pretty, is it?" said Vergie Propst, sipping on the Oodley Creek. "Here ya go", she said, "end of the line". Vergie Propst had stopped in front of one of the units; a loud voice was emanating from inside—-"Do you believe, do you believe?" someone was saying over and over, each time followed by a maniacal cackle.

"This is Polie's place, but you gotta understand that he's 'tetched in the head', not all the time, but plenty of the time," Vergie explained as she turned to leave. "Thanks for the shine, sugar," she said to Zeke as she sauntered away sipping on her cup, giving Zeke a lurid goodbye wink.

Zeke pulled the tattered blanket on the clothes line back and he and Cinnamon stepped inside the little open topped cubicle. Polie Maxwell was standing in front of them a few feet away with a long boney index finger thrust toward the sky. "Mr. Maxwell, I am Cinnamon, Harley Boylan's daughter, and this is my boyfriend Zeke. Could we come in and visit with you for a while?" Ginger asked, pursing her pretty pouty lips together.

"Yes children, come unto me as the children came unto Jesus. Have a seat on the cot while we chat," Polie said , grinning widely and exposing his vanishing dentition. Cinnamon and Zeke sat down on the grimy rickety cot that served as Polie Maxwell's bed. The esteemed former mayor was dressed in a tattered housecoat; it was threadbare and ragged strings hung from the worn sleeves. A colonel's ball cap, with the "scrambled eggs" on the front, sat cocked on his head. As Zeke Taylor looked at Polie he remembered the last time he had seen him, then a fit well dressed man sporting the raven haired Sister Alma around in a brand new Buick Roadmaster. As Zeke and Cinnamon watched the old man they soon learned that R.N. Vergie Propst's warning about Polie's mental meanderings were accurate.

"I was just remembering when back in 1947 I made the trip from Peru to French Polynesia. There were six of us in the craft, including Thor Heyerdahl. I gave ol' Thor the idea to name it the 'Kon Tiki'. It took us two days to lash that balsa wood together with jute," the former mayor proclaimed, looking off into the distance with his watery rheumy eyes. "Yep, it was a hell of a thing."

Cinnamon leaned over and whispered into Zeke's ear "who is this Thor guy?"

"I think it's some Norse god who hurls thunderbolts, but ain't sure baby. Damn, the nurse wuddn't lying about ol' Polie wuz she?" Zeke said. As they watched Polie Maxwell they saw his eyes change; the distant look left them and they seemed to clear a bit. He sat down on a straight backed chair. "Now what has brought you kids here today?" he asked, looking at the two of them.

"Well Mayor Maxwell, I don't know if you 'member me or not but I met you up at Boger City years ago at one of Sister Alma's revivals. I was one of them that she 'cured' that afternoon, along with Roger Haas,"

Zeke said, looking intently at Polie. Polie's eyes brightened at the mention of Sister Alma. "Oh yes, I do remember you—quite an act you had; how about doing that spastic twitching thing you did for her, just for old times sake." Without hesitation Zeke got up and lurched around the little cubicle, twitching his ass off.

"Yep," said Polie, laughing and slapping his knee. "That was one of the best performances I've ever seen, and that other boy was purty good too. What did you say his name was?".

"Roger Haas," replied Zeke.

"Sure, sure, I remember now, he was the boy that had the encounter with the watermelon up behind the drugstore one hot summer day," said Polie. "I remember it all now."

Zeke was amazed at how Polie Maxwell's mind could change gears, going from nonsense to crystal clarity. He figgered he would be there a while and would have to guide Polie Maxwell back to where he wanted him to go—to talk about Sister Alma. So Zeke gave it another try. "Mr. Maxwell, I came here today to see you because I want to be an evangelist, like Sister Alma was, and I am satisfied you knew her better than anybody, so I want to see if you can give me some insight into how sister Alma's mind worked, what made her so good, so persuasive, and how she could get people to believe in her," said Zeke. He hesitated to stop talking, fearing that Polie would go off on another nutty tirade, but Zeke had just run out of breath. His fears were quite justified.

As soon as Zeke Taylor paused in his entreaty Polie Maxwell jumped up from the straight backed chair, his eyes blazing, thrusting his boney right index finger skyward. "By God, you wanta know about Sister Alma, I'm gonna tell you about Sister Alma. She was the most beautiful and wild seductress ever to grace the bed of Polie Maxwell, and God Damn it I have had a plenty. She was the Exalted and Grand Cuntress of the land of Cunnilingua, and I was the King. She sat on her royal throne in the capital of Cunnilingua, the imperial city of Clitoria," Polie said, his eyes blazing wildly.

Zeke and Cinnamon looked at each other quizzically as Polie paused for a moment. "What is this country Cunnilingua?" Cinnamon asked Zeke. Zeke shrugged his shoulders and offered "I think it is somewhere in Europe, maybe 'round Lithuania."

Zeke took the opportunity of Polie Maxwell's momentary silence to try to get him back on topic.

"Mr. Maxwell," he said, "I know Sister Alma could almost hypnotize a crowd—and some say she did—and I know she had her beauty, and I know I ain't got none of that, but I swear I am sure I can be an evangelist, the same way Sister Alma was. I just need the insight and advice of the man who knew her best."

Polie Maxwell got up from the chair where he had rested while Zeke had his say and raised his eyes toward the ceiling and put his long arms in front of him and beckoned to Zeke Taylor. "Come to me, my son," Polie said, looking hard at Zeke. Zeke cautiously walked the few steps to where Polie Maxwell stood in his Colonel's cap with the scrambled eggs and his threadbare housecoat.

"Kneel down in front of me," Polie said, and when Zeke hesitated he shouted "NOW". Zeke immediately fell to his knees and Polie quickly reached into his pocket and placed something in his palm. "I now pronounce you to be The Prophet Ezekiel, and the right and true successor to Sister Alma," he said, and at that point placed his hand on Zeke Taylor's bowed head. Zeke jumped, quivered, and fell to the floor, as Polie Maxwell hollered and guffawed, slapping his knees. Cinnamon rushed to the fallen Zeke and helped him to his knees and then back over to the cot. The couple sat silently while Zeke recovered and listened to Polie talk.

"Ya see this thang," he said holding out a flat round object in his palm about the size of a fifty cent piece. "It's got a battery in it and will give out a purty good lil electrical charge, as you just felt Zeke. Sister Alma used it all the time and it brought many a sinner to Jesus."

Zeke was shaking his head and looking at Polie. "What was that all about Mr. Maxwell?" he asked, still trying to figger out what had happened. "What is all this about making me the successor to Sister Alma—I am confused?"

"Well son," Polie said, "when you started talking about how you wanted to be an evangelist, and when I remembered how you performed up there at Boger City with Sister Alma, I realized that you were serious and that you had what it took to do it." Polie had sat down in his chair and was smiling at Zeke and Cinnamon. "You know I have a lot of time on my hands in here, and I can't tell you how many times I have read the Bible, and with Zeke's name being what it is, it reminded me of a passage in the second chapter of the Book of Ezekiel, verse 5: "And they , whether they will hear, or whether they will forbear, (for they are a rebellious house) yet shall know that there hath been a prophet among them."

Polie Maxwell paused and looked at the shaken Zeke Taylor, really looked at him hard, but with a reassuring look on his haggard face. "I just needed to get your attention, Ezekiel. A good ol' electrical zap will do it every time, least that's what Sister Alma always said. Let me tell you a story 'bout this little buzzer. Back years ago when the ardent religious fathers of Dallas had built Sister Alma a 'tabernacle' down around the Court Square she would hold healing services every Saturday night, just like that one you were in at Boger City," Polie said, looking dead at Zeke with the penetrating stare he was capable of employing.

"Well it was rumored that Joe Clemmer, or Uncle Joe as he was commonly known, was gonna show up this particular night. The place was packed, 'cause Uncle Joe was purty much an icon around there, very well respected, and had always claimed that Sister Alma was a fake. Seems that Uncle Joe had a terrible case of arthritis in the back, in fact it was so bad that he walked all bent over. So as the rumor spread that he was coming for the 'cure' it of course caused quite a stir around town. I remember the whole night like it was yesterday. Sister Alma had delayed the healing service for a bit, hoping that Uncle Joe was really gonna show, 'cause she knew if she could do something with him she would have everybody in her back pocket. To kill time she got Chief Usher Elmer and his assistants to take up a 'love offering'——-she felt okay about doing this 'cause it had been a good three months since the last one. Alma always cautioned about appearing greedy; four love offerings a year was her limit. Anyway, the love offering had been taken up and dumped in the tin tub at the front of the stage. I remember very well the last usher to empty his plate; it was Pasour Rhyne, the crazy son of a bitch that killed my beloved Alma—-may he rot in hell."

Zeke, who had pretty much recovered from his "shock", and Cinnamon had been listening intently to Polie Maxwell and were taken aback when he raised his voice in condemning Pasour Rhyne. As they watched the former mayor they saw him get that wild and crazy look in his eyes again. They figgered something was comin'.

Polie Maxwell rose quickly from his straight backed chair and stood bolt upright. He reached into his tattered housecoat and pulled something out, quickly applying it to his upper lip. Polie turned away and then faced Zeke and Cinnamon quickly, grinning congenially; he was sporting a small mustache.

"Now contestants," he said , doing his best Alex Trebek inpersonation, "the next category is rhyme time. The $200.00 answer is 'Fallacious Fellator'. Polie looked at them expectantly and then said' and the question is 'What is a lying cocksucker?" Polie heehawed and pranced around the tiny cubicle as Zeke Taylor and Cinnamon Boylan stared at each other. After a bit Cinnamon remembered something her Daddy had told her and leaned closely to Zeke's ear; "Daddy said he is a big jeopardy fan", she said. They sat watching Polie pull off and re-apply the mustache. "Now you see it, now you don't," Zeke looked quizzically at Cinnamon; Cinnamon, a frequent watcher of Jeopardy herself, explained that Alex Trebek went back and forth frequently on having a mustache and shaving it off. The couple sat in silence, Zeke figgering that ol' Polie would have a "clear spell" eventually. After a minute Polie looked at Zeke and said "You are nowThe Prophet Ezekiel, and that is the name you are to go by from this day forward if you want my help . I am going to tell you the secret of being a successful evangelist."

Zeke and Cinnamon looked at Polie Maxwell curiously; his eyes had cleared up again, and he was back to his old self. "The secret is sex, hot assed sex appeal, and Zeke, you are a good looking boy and a charmer, and you can pull it off—-you will have the women falling all over you and opening up their pocketbooks, and 'bout anything else they got," Polie said, grinning knowingly at Zeke. But you need a counterpart to entice the men, and she is sittin' right beside you."

Zeke and Cinnamon stared at each other for a good thirty seconds before they truly realized what Polie Maxwell was saying. Neither of them had ever thought for a minute that Cinnamon would be involved in the evangelistic endeavor. Finally Zeke broke the silence, looking at the paternalistic former mayor—-at least that was the way he was acting at the time.

"Mayor Maxwell, you mean you think Cinnamon ought to be on the stage with me, preaching and everything?" a slightly confused Zeke asked Polie Maxwell. "Yes son," Polie replied, his demeanor now becoming so incredibly smooth and confident. "Cinnamon is a smart girl so she could pick up on what to do. She might not have that innate showmanship talent you have but I am sure those behaviors can be learned. And of course her physical attributes are apparent and abundant." At this Cinnamon giggled, then pursed those pouty lips, batted her eyelashes and said "Well I guess you might maybe be right about that Mayor Maxwell," grinning at Polie and thrusting her shoulders back. "34 double D?" Polie queried, giggling at his naughtiness. "Ya know Alma was a double D; My God they were fantastic!" Polie's eyes clouded over for a moment and Zeke thought maybe he was gonna go nuts again, but they cleared up quickly as Polie offered "I'll tell you Ezekiel, you get the one-two punch of y'all workin, and you would be hard to beat. I know I am right; Alma knew that being by herself limited her somewhat, and one time she even tried to get me on the stage but I just couldn't do it. I been in politics most of my life, and I got no problem talking to a crowd, but all this faith healin' and praying and everything, I just couldn't get into it. But the two of you could pull it off. Ya just need to get Cinnamon some long, slinky dresses with a split up the side and a plunging neck line to show them things off and the two of you will be unbeatable."

Zeke sat contemplating this new wrinkle of Cinnamon sort of being a partner; at first he didn't quite know what to think, but the more he sat there and thought about it the more he liked it. Cinnamon was also in a contemplative mood; she was thinking about the only time she had ever seen Sister Alma in action. It happened when she was sixteen years old and was riding around one night with of a couple of girl friends drinking beer when they happened to ride by Sister Alma's "Tabernacle" and on a whim went inside to see what was going on. Cinnamon remembered seeing the gorgeous, raven haired, bosomy beauty prancing around on the stage in a red sequined tight fitting dress that went to the floor but had a slit up the left side all the way to between her knee and her hip. Cinnamon recalled how Sister Alma would bound about on the stage, and how her tethered breasts would bounce. She thought about her own endowment, looking down at them, and at that point came to the realization that she could pull it off.

Zeke looked at Cinnamon and gave her his sneaky, sly wink that had made her fall in love and in bed with him when she was only sixteen. "Whaddaya think baby?" he said, grinning at his woman. "In for a penny, in for a friggin' kilogram," she said, smiling the beautiful smile with the tumescent lips framing the perfect teeth. Zeke grabbed Cinnamon's hand and together they stood; Polie Maxwell stood also and gave both of them a big hug, smiling broadly and placing a hand on each of their heads. Then he solemnly pronounced "Go and sin no more." Ezekiel and Cinnamon pulled back the blanket hanging on the wire and exited the cubicle; the last words they heard from Polie Maxwell were "and if you truly believe in the theory of relativity and couch that theory in the space and time continuum"............. Polie Maxwell's voice trailed off as they headed out of the large room and passed through the French doors into the vestibule where Vergie Propst, R. N., was sitting behind her desk. They stopped there and Ezekiel The Prophet opened the Oodley and filled her cup, placing his hand on her orange hair and saying "Go and sin no more." Vergie took a long drink, smiled, and said "fat fuckin' chance of that sugar."

Part 3—SHOWTIME

Six months had passed since The Prophet Ezekiel and Cinnamon had visited the former mayor Polie Maxwell at the County Home, and it had been two months since they had attended his simple funeral service out at Philadelphia Church, the Lutheran church outside of town where Polie Maxwell had sometimes attended. Although his lifestyle typically precluded his being an early riser on Sundays, he was still on the books as a member and entitled to a plot in the large cemetery adjacent to the little country church. The circumstances of the late Mayor's demise were not widely known, but a trip by the Prophet Ezekiel where he brought along a quart of fresh Oodley Creek greased the wheels and tongue of Nurse Vergie Propst and halfway through the second cup of the refreshing elixir The Prophet Ezekiel had the story.

The two of them were in the anteroom at the County Home where Vergie's desk was; she propped her chubby legs covered with the white stockings up on the desk, grinning at The Prophet as he quickly noted that the Registered Nurse had not bothered to don any underwear. The Prophet quickly averted his eyes and Vergie told the story.

"Well the Mayor was having a really boisterous day—-had never seen him so wild. I had gone into his area three times in as many hours to try to quiet him down, but it didn't seem to do any good. Then on in the afternoon after I had returned from lunch one of the attendants came to me and said that Polie Maxwell was missing, that they had looked all over and could not find him. We continued to search the place and then I noticed that in my absence the locked door that shut off the stairway had been pried open. About that time we heard a big commotion out in the room, the one where Polie's cubicle was. When we got out there everybody was kinda looking up toward the ceiling. The barricaded stairway led to an open walkway, kind of like you would see in the old westerns in the saloons; there was a railing but it was open above, with a carved post about every ten feet. Rooms that were not used anymore led off the walkway. Perched up on the railing was Polie Maxwell, naked as a jaybird except for his tattered colonel's cap with the scrambled eggs on the front.

He was hollerin' and laughin' and shoutin' some nonsense about his buddy Charles A. Lindbergh and bout how 'The Spirit of Saint Louis' was about to enter. Polie was hanging on to the post, still balancing on the top of the rail when he lifted his wild eyes toward the ceiling and shouted 'In comes one spirit and out goes another', and with that pitched headlong off the railing and landed on the floor. Luckily he did not hit anyone else, but he was quite dead, his broken neck almost completely turned around from the front of his body, but his wild crazy eyes remaining fully open."

The six months since Zeke, or The Prophet Ezekiel as he was now known, and Cinnamon had visited the late mayor had been pretty active. The first thing Zeke Taylor did was legally change his name to "The Prophet Ezekiel". When Zeke had decided to do this he went to see the attorney who had represented him several times, Perry Markis, and got some advice. He found out that it was a pretty simple procedure, not even requiring an attorney, and out of the goodness of his heart Perry Markis gave Zeke the lowdown on how to proceed. Barrister Markis was known to do a lot of pro bono work like this; unfortunately, many times the situation didn't start out being pro bono, it just wound up that way after the local riffraff wouldn't pay up. Anyway, Perry Markis tole Zeke" to submit a written application, stating your current name, place of birth and residence, as well at the name you would like to adopt and the reason why you are seeking to change your name." Perry told him to sign and date the document and file it with the Clerk of Court, paying the fee at the time of filing. Then all one had to do was wait to be notified of a hearing date, attend the hearing, and answer any questions that the Judge may have for him. Perry explained that these hearings were typically routine and that it was rare for a judge to have a question; however, when Judge John W. Bulwinkle read the legal name change request before him on the day of Zeke Taylor's hearing he could not help being a bit curious. Judge Bulwinkle had been on the bench for over thirty years and in that time had presided over a handful of name change petitions, usually having to do with adoptions and such mundane activities, but he had never seen anything quite like the request before him that afternoon in The Gaston County Court House. To add a little further spice in the situation Zeke Taylor had appeared before His Honor several times for a range of infractions; in fact, Judge Bulwinkle was the one who had sentenced Zeke to six months less than a year ago."

"Mr. Taylor," the Judge boomed, looking over the top of his little reading glasses, a favorite act of intimidation adopted by many of his ilk, "Why is it that you want to change your name to 'The Prophet Ezekiel?" Zeke calmly stood up and told Judge Bulwinkle how his time in prison had changed his life and that he had decided that he wanted to be an evangelist, that he knew it would be his life's work, and that his wife, Cinnamon Boylan, was going to assist him in the endeavor. As usual, once Zeke got to talking he would get on a roll, the momentum building, and before you knew it Zeke's eyes had teared up and he had confessed to Judge Bulwinkle that he owed him a considerable debt for sending him away. "Your honor, I wanta thank you for doin' what you did, for I was indeed on the wrong path, and my time in prison allowed me to examine myself like never before, and thus come to realize my true destiny." Having heard that Judge Bulwinkle grinned wryly, shook his head, and pronounced "Petition is approved".

The Prophet Ezekiel then thanked the Judge, the Prophet's request to have a word of prayer falling by the wayside as Judge Bulwinkle quickly exited the courtroom, still shaking his head.

Choking back a little disappointment at not being able to lead the courtroom in communication with God, The Prophet Ezekiel quickly recovered, picked up his bona fide legal paperwork and headed home to Cinnamon Boylan and their single wide trailer that her father had set them up in a few months before they had tied the knot. The Prophet Ezekiel and his woman had never really talked seriously about getting married, but after the meeting with Polie Maxwell and the evangelical decision they began to discuss it and decided that if they were going to present themselves in a proper light they had better get legit. So it came to pass that the couple came to be united in holy matrimony in Cinnamon's parents' back yard one Sunday afternoon. It was a small affair, the two of them agreeing to each invite a couple of friends and leave it at that. The Prophet Ezekiel invited Woodrow Royal, an old run around friend of his and Steve Hall, a fellow he had known since young childhood. Cinnamon invited Janice Brinkman, who had grown up next door to her, and Montana Morton, her best friend in high school. Janice Brinkman was known as the "Widder Brinkman" around town, although she was not yet twenty years old. She had received the moniker because she had refused to even date any guy ever since her husband Dickie had died on the night of their wedding. The nuptials had been prompted by a late period, a diagnosis of pregnancy, a quick visit by her father to her boyfriend Dickie Brinkman's house, a discussion with him and his parents, and a very quick wedding, like the next day. So after Janice's Daddy's visit, and his proclamation that he was sporting a ".32 caliber pistol in the back pocket of my overalls" all of the Brinkman clan quickly agreed that a matrimonial union was the way to go. The elder Brinkman was a member of St. Paul's Lutheran Church over around Harden and he was able to secure the church the next afternoon, which fortuitously was a Sunday. The minister of the church was on vacation and this put the group into a panic until someone remembered that the local high school had hired a new teacher and that he was an ordained minister, albeit in the Baptist Church. Under the extreme circumstances this variation was "overlooked", and the Right Reverend Lee Barron was called late Saturday afternoon and after some nominal dickering agreed to perform the service for fifteen dollars. The Reverend Barron had just been hired as a physical education teacher, his large belly and bulbous ass making it hard to believe he had ever done the first pushup; moreover, the popular football coach having left for the big time in a 4A conference and no one else willing to assume the gridiron reins, Lee Barron was offered the job of head football coach. He accepted right away, the extra money looking pretty good since he had just managed to impregnate his "Olive Oyl" lookalike wife. "Thank God for those hormone shots you took," his wife had exclaimed to Lee. Lee Barron had never coached football in his life; Lee Barron had never played football in his life.

Lee Barron's ministerial career had gotten off to a less than enthusiastic welcome from the local populace. He had substituted at several Baptist churches the past summer when the regular ministers were on vacation. The flocks had a little difficulty getting accustomed to his strange vocal

THE PROPHET EZEKIEL

inflections; the Reverend Barron had a naturally high squeaky voice in normal speech but when he would lead them in prayer he would switch gears, a basso profundo boom emanating from his chubby jowls—-it was sorta like going from Mickey Mouse to George Beverly Shea at warp speed.

As the small group gathered in the Boylan backyard that afternoon there was a less than exciting air about. Woodrow Royal had already pinched the Widder Brinkman on her ample ass and had been rewarded with a hard slap.. The Widder had pretty much soured on life in general, never being able to get past the death of her husband on their wedding day After the ceremony the couple had retired to the T&M Motel, up on the hill behind Tommy's Drive In. Tommy's was known for delicious sliced BBQs and thick milkshakes; the T&M was known for cheap rates and the availability of prostitutes. It was what the young couple could afford, and after they went in their room and got settled, Janice putting on her new black negligee, Dickie decided he would run out to Don Moose's to get a coupla half pints of liquor. Don Moose had a single wide trailer out past Philadelphia Lutheran Church, and he sold a variety of alcohol which he bought legally in South Carolina and then re-sold illegally out of his trailer. It was obvious where the half pints came from, for Gaston County was dry and you could not buy half pints anywhere in North Carolina. So instead of going to Charlotte to buy his supplies, Mr. Moose went across the border to Clover, South Carolina , the half pints being a most popular size. Don Moose did a brisk business, especially in the underage male category. The half pints sold very well, Bourbon De Luxe and Popov vodka being the most popular. As Dickie Brinkman, excited newlywed, made his way down Philadelphia Church Road to the bootlegger he was trying to decide which one he wanted, the Bourbon or the Vodka, but once he got inside the trailer and saw the glistening bottles he decided to get one of each, figgering he would kill one of them on the ride back to the T&M.

Dickie Brinkman carried the two bags out to his Kelly Green Mach 1 Mustang and tore out of the rutted driveway, unscrewing the top of the Popov Vodka bottle. Dickie loved to drive fast, and loved to drink fast, and was purty good at both. Two miles down the road the empty Popov bottle was lying in the passenger seat and the Mach 1 was doin' 110. At least that's what the N. C. Highway Patrolman estimated his speed when he hit the side of the steel bridge spanning the South Fork River and went airborne, hitting a venerable oak about fifteen feet up before falling back to earth and rolling into the river. So the newlywed widow never got over it and turned bitter and sad—thus Woodrow Royal's ringing cheeks.

It was time for the wedding and everyone was there except the preacher. Money being a bit tight The Prophet Ezekiel had secured the services of the Reverend Lee Barron, still the cheapest around although inflation had elevated his fee to $20.00. Finally the Reverend motivated his bulbous ass into the Boylan back yard, motioning The Prophet Ezekiel to stand aside for a moment. Once they were alone the Reverend explained that he now required payment in advance, having been burned by the wedding of Dickie brinkman and the very Widder who was standing nearby. Dickie had promised Reverend Barron to bring him the $15.00 the next day, that appointment having been interrupted ty the southeast corner of the South Fork River bridge. "One never knows, do one," Reverend Lee Barron said to The Prophet Ezekiel as he grinned and licked his thick lips, quickly tucking the twenty dollar bill in his size 44 pants pocket.

Reverend Lee Barron began the service, using his normal squeaky Mickey Mouse voice, until the very end, when he called the group to prayer with his deep bass roll, sounding a bit more like a bullfrog than George Beverly Shea. "Dear Eternal Father, giver of all life, to you and your risen son Jesus Christ we offer up our prayers for this young couple, Cinnamon Boylan and The Prophet Ezekiel".

"The Prophet Ezekiel was watching the Reverend Lee Barron closely, and could almost swear that he saw a little derisive eye roll when the Reverend said the words "The Prophet Ezekiel", but the former Zeke Taylor had never liked the son of a bitch anyway, so since he couldn't tell for sure he just let it go Eventually "Froggy Shea" finished, the crowd dispersed, and The Prophet Ezekiel took a quick honeymoon trip to Carolina Beach with his bride, returning the next afternoon——The Prophet Ezekiel had a lot of work to do.

Since the pivotal meeting with the late Polie Maxwell and the advice that he had imparted to Zeke Taylor and Cinnamon Boylan, both of the aspiring evangelists had been very busy. After they had left the County home that afternoon Zeke and Cinnamon had headed to The Meadowbrook Supper Club, where they had gone when Zeke had got out of prison. It was a comfortable place to talk and the food was as good as ever, so they got cheeseburgers and long necked "Blues in a Bottle" and set to planning. It was at this point that Zeke divulged to Cinnamon his idea of legally changing his name to "The Prophet Ezekiel". He also clued Cinnamon in to the plan he had for her, which had been suggested by Polie Maxwell. Zeke Taylor had put a lot of stock into what Polie had told them, and as crazy as he could be Zeke believed that Polie Maxwell was onto something. Polie's idea that Cinnamon Boylan accompany "The Prophet Ezekiel" in the evangelical endeavor was intriguing to Zeke Taylor and he was very excited about patterning Cinnamon after the late Sister Alma. "It will work, sugarpie, trust me on this. After we get rolling people will start remembering her because you will remind them of her, at least physically. I know you are not a big talker like I am, but early on you can be more of an 'eye candy' attraction. We'll get you some slinky long dresses with a slit up the thigh and you can play that role until you get more comfortable with the program. Then you can start preaching a little; I know we can make it work."

As usual Cinnamon had fallen in lockstep with Zeke's idea, and for the six months since the County Home visit she had very willingly gone along with Zeke's leadership, from the legal name change, to the first purchase of an appropriate gown for Cinnamon; additionally, the newly named "The Prophet Ezekiel" had tied six bed sheets together and suspended them about eight feet in the air in the back yard, supported by saplings The Prophet had cut out of the woods behind their trailer. The Prophet was working every day, really hard, but he spent a couple of hours every night in his "tent", reading the Bible out loud, shouting out phrases like "Can you feel the spirit," "Are you gonna let him in your heart," and "Get down on your knees and pray to God and Jesus Christ to loose the demons from your soul so that you can truly be saved and have everlasting life, which your Lord and Savior died on the cross to give you."

The Prophet Ezekiel, being the natural showman that he was (as recognized and proclaimed by the late Polie Maxwell), purty much fed on himself during these monologues; he paid attention to the timbre of his voice, and having watched plenty of Sunday morning preachers on television and having heard Sister Alma in person, he had a plethora to emulate and draw from. The Prophet had also grown up listening to the small local radio stations; every Sunday in the a.m. WGAS, "the flagship station of Gaston County," would turn over its 20,000 watt broadcaster to a bunch of Free Will Baptists from Bessemer City, and The Prophet would tune them in religiously. The Prophet Ezekiel, then known as Zeke Taylor, would really get off on the ministers; he called them "wheezers". The Prophet really liked their very predictable cadence; he didn't give a shit about the message, but he got a kick out of the way they delivered it. His favorite by far was Zeno Carpenter, a farmer by trade who hailed from up near Bethel Church. The Prophet had actually met Zeno Carpenter and thought of him as a regular little humble dirt farmer, until he heard his ass on the radio. Zeno had the best and most vibrant voice of the WGAS guest preachers, and his delivery went something like this—————"And you know Jesus loves you, and he is watching over you, and he died for your sins, and there is no hope for you without him, and he died on the cross, and his body was mutilated, and they put him in the tomb, and then they found the rock rolled away, and he was gone, and he was ascended to heaven to forever be on the right hand of the Lord," and on and on and on and on and on and on and on.

The Prophet called then "wheezers" because every one of them would get into that rhythm and take a huge breath before each phrase, expending so much energy during each recitation that they would have to take another huge breath for the next phrase; their intake of air was so pronounced that it actually sounded like a wheeze, and thus The Prophet's name for them.

But Zeno Carpenter was the "Wheezer King" and The Prophet hung on his every word and even mimicked Zeno when he was out drinking beer and smoking dope with his buddies when he was a teenager.

The Prophet Ezekiel felt like he had pretty fertile ministerial soil to help him cultivate his nascent evangelism; he had also been working on his praying technique. He had seen and heard many a mediocre sermon saved by a whiz bang ending prayer, so The Prophet paid a lot of attention to this. The Prophet also was tuned in to the necessity of being flexible in delivery and style of praying and knowing when to be benign and when to "call on the Everlasting and Abundant Spirit of Jesus Christ, Our Savior, who bled and died on the cross to save us sorry people, so that we can be in heaven in the by and by."

The Prophet Ezekiel had written down what he considered "a purty good attempt" at a sort of prayer that one might offer at a gathering of friends or family——the kind of situation where you really did not want to sound too "churchified". It went like this: "Whether by design or happenstance we are gathered here today. If a supreme being has sheltered us from harm over the last year, more power to Him or Her and we pay homage to He, She, or It. If that not be the case, then we are no worse for the wear, for in reality most of us have no clue as to why we are here and what we are destined to do. But I have faith in the following; we are a group who have love and respect for each other, enjoy each other's company, and so look forward to seeing each other . To this let us raise our glasses. Salud."

The Prophet had practiced this prayer a lot out under his sheet tabernacle, and had even used it a couple of times in live settings, and had gotten good reviews. At one gathering where a dog had chased a beloved cat up a tree The Prophet had customized his benign prayer. The gathering was a group of about twenty friends and neighbors and all was going well until the hostess' grey tabby, Carlton, escaped the house and was chased up a tree by a mixed breed dog named Batman. Carlton the cat was no foreigner to adversity, being a rescue kitty from the mean streets of Orange County, so he knew what to do, the end result being his watching Batman and the gathered crowd from thirty feet up a tulip magnolia tree. The hostess' sister didn't help a lot, offering "well I've always heard that cats can climb up okay but they have a lot of trouble getting down." Then someone else chimed in with "Yep, Cindy's cat stayed up in a tree for three days." Fortunately the panic stricken owner, a nice retired lady named Roberta, was out of earshot and was spared these dire predictions, and ol'

Carlton decided to come down after only an hour and a half. Well it was getting close to meal time and The Prophet Ezekiel knew that he would be called upon for the blessing, so he decided to "personalize" it a bit and vary his typical generic offering. So when the time came he began plastering his best attempt at a beatific smile on his handsome face and proceeded: "What a wonderful occasion we have today, this gathering of friends, lovers, and family. (His mention of lovers drew a titter from some of the couples who lived together without being married.) As we look about this room (his head rotating as he spoke these words) we realize the abundance of love and respect we share with each other. And finally, I would like to recite a few time honored phrases that I feel appropriate——Home is the hunter, home from the hill, and the sailor home from the sea"——(at this point he paused for a good ten seconds, long enough for people to start looking around at each other, wondering about this odd blessing) but then with what The Prophet felt was perfect timing he added "And Carlton the Cat, thank God, is down from the tree." The Prophet Ezekiel received the response he was looking for, as the entire group erupted in raucous laughter, Roberta laughing the loudest as she cuddled her beloved Carlton.

But although The Prophet was extremely busy practicing prayers and sermon ideas in his tent tabernacle he did not forget the people he had met in prison, some of whom he had become pretty good friends with. He had kept a letter from one of them, a guy named Mikey, that he had received around Christmas after The Prophet had been released. The Prophet had sent Mikey ten dollars for spending money in the prison canteen, and The Prophet had received the following letter: "Hello to my family of friends! Thank you for all you have did for me over the past few years. And a special thanks to the one that has got you all together, doing the wonderful things you all have did for me! I'm blessed to have friend's like you. The card state's friend but no, it is FRIENDS! Marry Christmas."

The Prophet Ezekiel always smiled when he read this letter from Mikey; it made him realize a couple of things; one was that no matter what people had done and how they had wound up they were still human beings and usually would respond well to a little affection and a few bucks, and the other was that Mikey could have stood a little overtime in English class. But The Prophet understood all of this, and even forgave Mikey for sending him a generic letter instead of personalizing it. Mikey had bigger worries, not being eligible for parole for ten years being one of them.

The Prophet also had gotten to where he would fantasize about potential events and how he would handle them, all of these ideas revolving around the time when The Prophet Ezekiel would launch his evangelistic ship. One of these recurring notions involved the Honorable Judge Bulwinkle, the very one who had sentenced The Prophet to prison and had then recently granted him his change of moniker. The Prophet could hold a grudge, and the fact that the Judge had departed the courtroom so abruptly, forestalling the Prophet's attempt at prayer, had, to put it mildly, stuck in The Prophet Ezekiel's evangelistic craw. The fantasy was the Judge Bulwinkle would have passed away, and The Prophet would be at his funeral at Christ Episcopal Church, the closest thing to a blue blood country club church that Gastonia had to offer. The eulogy would have been delivered and the attending Rector, although it was not usually done in the Episcopal Church, would have decided that because of the beloved Judge's stature in the community that he would invite people to stand up and say something about Judge Bulwinkle. Rector William Doub Stinnett would have realized he was taking a little bit of a chance, this type of "communal eulogizing" being more common in a Methodist or Baptist venue, but would have decided to do it anyway. Rector Stinnett would even have thought that it might have a bit of entertainment value, but he would never have admitted that to anyone.

So it came to pass that The Prophet Ezekiel went over this imagined scenario in his mind endlessly and came up with what he felt like would be the perfect eulogy to be delivered if such an eventuality occurred. The Prophet knew exactly what he would do——he would wait patiently while some of the town fathers spoke grandiloquently of the late Judge Bulwinkle and then he would get the attention of Rector Stinnett and be recognized. First he would stand and look all around the large sanctuary, making eye contact with as many luminaries as possible and then begin to speak.

"Most Revered and Right Rector Stinnett, I thank you from the bottom of my most grateful heart to have this opportunity to speak of our dear departed Judge Rockford Bulwinkle. For those of you who may not know me I am The Prophet Ezekiel, formerly known as Zeke Taylor, but I have shed that name, as a snake sheds its skin, and am now legally The Prophet Ezekiel, our honored departed Judge having presided over the legal procedure. And I am here to tell you of the wisdom of our departed friend, for he played such an important part in my life". At this point The Prophet imagined that he would again look around at the gathered mourners, nodding and smiling at everyone, but paying special attention to the city powers. Then having assured himself that he most certainly had their undivided attention, he would continue.

"I am satisfied that many of you do not know of me, having never heard of me, but I will tell you one man who knew me, and that would be Judge Rockford Bulwinkle. And he may have known me better than any other man, or maybe I just think so because he had such an influence over me. Please indulge me for a few moments as I relate this story to you". The Prophet would pause and look over the mourning crowd, numbering at least two hundred. He could tell that his request was indeed rhetorical, for he definitely had their attention.

"Now, my people",he began. The Prophet Ezekiel totally knew he was going way out on a limb using this verbage, but he had a feeling, and when he got a feeling, the showman came to the forefront and he decided to let it roll. "Let me tell you what our dear departed Judge Bulwinkle did for me, how he saved me, from MYSELF, and how he essentially performed a miracle for this poor lil ol' country boy from Dallas, North Carolina, zip code 28034. As The Prophet spoke these words he would look around and see that he was making inroads, his dark tan and perfect dentition being a definite plus, for as he surveyed the crowd he could see that the females were riveted on his presence, and many were smiling adoringly.

"Yes, people, I have not been a paradigm of virtue in my life time, this I freely admit. And I have had some scrapes with the authorities, and I will tell you that I appeared before our passed brother Judge on several occasions, and I can elaborate and tell you this——the Honorable Judge Rockford Bulwinkle ALWAYS, ALWAYS, treated me fairly, and went out of his way to do so".

As The Prophet repeated ALWAYS twice he would raise his voice to nearly a shout, disturbing the dozing Hub Carpenter on the back aisle. Hub Carpenter would respong with a loud "Amen", which he always did when roused from a nap. Hub's enjoinder would be quickly responded to by The Prophet; "Yes brother, say it again", he would say, to which Hub would shout back "Amen", even louder, and The Prophet would notice more than a few of the adoring females joining in with a murmur of "amens". As The Prophet's eyes would roam the parishioners he would see some of the men starting to nod in agreement. The Prophet Ezekiel knew that this was a huge inroad, for he would be well aware of how staid and conservative this Episcopalian bunch tended to be.

But The Prophet's eyes would not be the only set scanning the group; Rector William Doub Stinnett would have picked up on the building excitement. Although the good Rector faithfully delivered the kind of benign pabulum characteristic of the Episcopalians, what with all of their readings and Pseudo-Catholic raiment, the Rector did appreciate a good show, and he would feel like he was getting ready to witness one. The tune "Can I get a witness, can I get a witness" would be dancing through his head, this mood being enhanced by the two Double Scotches he downed back in his office just prior to the service. "Oh well," he would think to himself, "as the old axiom goes, if you find four Episcopalians gathered you are sure to find a fifth." He would actually chuckle when he thought these words, but would quickly recover and put his gaze back on The Prophet.

"And I can also tell you this, brothers and sisters, the Late Departed Honorable Judge Bulwinkle gave me a new lease on life, and an insight into my destiny, and if you will allow me I will share this story with you". At this moment The Prophet would pause, purposely , and look around the sanctuary, observing with great pleasure the nods of assurance. The Prophet would continue.

"The beginning of the defining period of my life occurred when he Judge sentenced me to six months in prison, and I am her to tell you it could easily have been twice that much if not for his well known leniency." The Prophet, in his fantasy, would then recount his time in prison, his "moment of truth" in solitary, and his aspirations, telling the group that he would soon be on the evangelical landscape and to watch out for him "cause I got something to say". Then as his imaginings came to a close the sanctuary would be filled with "amens" and "God bless yous" and the Right Rector would have a bit of an envious and concerned look on his face.

The Prophet Ezekiel practiced all of his prayers and evangelical "shout outs" and fantasy speeches endlessly in his tent tabernacle. On occasion he would pretend that the small trees outside the tent in his back yard were "the faithful", and would point at them and exhort them to "come clean to Jesus Christ and the Glorious Gospel and let The Prophet Ezekiel be the Holy Vessel through which you are cleansed and sanctified."

Eventually he brought Cinnamon within the fold of his Tent Tabernacle. The Prophet had her dress up in her new slinky dress with red sequins and a long slit up the side of her left leg that ended halfway up her thigh. The beautiful dress was complemented by her gorgeous "blasting blue" eyes and the package was topped off by her bounteous breasts, her gown dipping deep in the front to reveal some serious cleavage. The Prophet Ezekiel brought Cinnamon along slowly, the first few times just having her stand near him and smile while she held a tambourine that he had bought for her. Then he secured a couple of tapes of religious songs, selecting the ol' staples "Bringing In The Sheaves", "Just As I Am", and "Shall We Gather At The River". The Prophet remembered that Sister Alma had used these songs on a regular basis and that it had appeared to be very effective. "Just As I Am" and "Shall We Gather At The River" were really good "closers", saved for the end of the service, when the collection plates would be distributed and a hopefully inspired crowd would open their hearts and wallets to further the nascent evangelistic endeavors of The Prophet and his beautiful mate. "The Sheaves" was more of a seasonal song which he would bring in during the fall harvesting, for Gaston County folk either worked in the fields or the cotton mills or both.

So The Prophet continued to practice his delivery and the many nuances of his glorious trade. To make the scene more realistic he decided to enlarge the tent and give it more height; he accomplished this by substituting taller saplings for the existing supports and stringing together more sheets. Then he got Willie Cline to climb up the big oak tree in the back yard with a come along and a rope tied to the top of the tent. Willie ratcheted the top of the tent up in the air and tied it off, giving The Prophet a circle about 16' wide in the center of the complex that reached a height of twelve feet at the peak. When the enlargement was finished the tent virtually filled the back yard of the trailer, and amazingly The Prophet noticed a smattering of people dropping by each night, a group that increased until one night he looked up and counted 20 people sitting on the grass or just standing around watching him practice. The Prophet just kept to his regimen, reviewing sermon topics, practicing the favored hymns, showcasing Cinnamon, and once in a while trying his hand at a prophecy or two. The Prophet was cautious in this endeavor, as he knew that by his name people were going to expect certain things from him, but he didn't want to rush headlong into it, preferring to be careful. The Prophet Ezekiel had noticed over the past few weeks that Willie Cline's addled fat sister with orange hair, Tina, or "Teener" as she was known, had had several brushes with near disaster. The Clines lived on Highway 321, known as "Killer 321" by a local newspaperman, and "Teener" walked back and forth on the side of the road, usually going down to "Bill's Food Center" to get candy or going to see her Aunt Lucy who was equally fat and addled. Taking all this into account The Prophet made an announcement at the end of his practice session one night. "Ladies and gentlemen", he said looking at the roughly 25 potential parishioners milling about, "I have an announcement to make' no, this is actually a prophecy". At the mention of this magical word all conversation in the makeshift tent venue ceased, all eyes being riveted on The Prophet. The Prophet had summoned the lovely Cinnamon to his side, where she stood solemnly holding her tambourine.

"As you all know," he said, "I am The Prophet Ezekiel, that is my legal name, and you also know that I am an 'evangelist in training." A murmur of "yes, we know," and "please go on," could be heard through the group. .

"Well it is time for my first prophesy: within one week Killer 321 will claim another life". The group gasped as one, and watched as The Prophet Ezekiel turned quickly and went into his trailer, the lovely Cinnamon on his heels. Once they were inside The Prophet explained to Cinnamon that the abrupt departure was for effect and told her what he had noticed about

"Teener." Cinnnamon wondered out loud if they shouldn't try to do something to help the poor girl but The Prophet cut her short.

"Cinnamon," he said, "everybody and his brother have told that dumb bitch to stay well off the road instead of hugging the shoulder like she does; it just falls on deaf ears. Bottom line, honey, is you just can't fix stupid." This explanation satisfied her and she dropped it, Cinnamon not being the type to ponder things at length. It was kind of like the time that Cinnamon got the great idea that the local KKK Klavern might be a fertile area for The Prophet to delve into. Although the KKK did have a modest membership in the area The Prophet Ezekiel patiently explained that they were a bit extreme for most people and that it would not be a very wise idea. Cinnamon quickly agreed, and after thinking about those funny hats they wore decided that abandoning the idea was indeed for the best 'cause that goofy hat would play hell with her perfectly coiffed hair style.

More and more people started showing up at The Prophet's nightly practices, which he considered to be a true blessing. The Prophet thought it a great opportunity to showcase his talents in a very low pressure setting. But there was a downside to the burgeoning crowd and it came to light one evening about seven thirty when Doug Huffmeister showed up. Huffmeister was a county building inspector and The Prophet Ezekiel, and 'bout everybody else in construction in Gaston County despised him. The Prophet's disdain for him revolved around Huffmeister shaking down the fencing company he worked for on a regular basis. Huffmeister would just show up on a job site, sporting his little dinky building inspector badge on his belt and find something wrong with the fence——-either it would be too tall or a few inches over the line or something. Then Doug Huffmeister would say "well you know it's gotta come down" or some such nonsense. All the contractors in the county knew the routine; and an envelope with three twenty dollar bills in it always fomented Huffmeister's quick departure.

So when The Prophet saw the Inspector he knew what to expect, especially when he saw that Huffmeister had somehow secured an additional badge, so he had one attached to each side of his belt, Gaston County's fabled spindle emblem emblazoned in the center of the badges. The bobbin represented the textile industry, the largest employer in the area. The Prophet Ezekiel stopped his scripture reading and walked over to where the Inspector was standing with his thumbs stuck under his belt which secured an ample beer belly.

"Whatcha doin' here Zekey Boy?" Huffmeister asked, showing a gap toothed grin and gazing at The Prophet through his little piggy eyes.

"Inspector Huffmeister, you need to know that I have legally changed my name to The Prophet Ezekiel and that I am an evangelist in training; you can verify this through county legal records or by calling Judge Bulwinkle, but I require of you that I be addressed by my proper name." Huffmeister chuckled. "Okay, The Prophet Ezekiel, we got us a little problem here. What we got is what in the building code is called an Assembly Occupancy, and when ya got one of them they's a bunch of hoops to jump through." Inspector Huffmeister stopped talking in order to let this very official sounding verbage sink in. The Prophet just looked at the gloating Inspector for a minute and then asked "So what does this Assembly Occupancy involve?".

Inspector Huffmeister started strutting around and looking at everything. "Well you have all these safety precautions involved, like proper exits and handicap accessibility, including ramps and handrails, and ya gotta look at these sheets for what their flame spread index is——-why, I bet they ain't even got one. I 'magine a thrown away cigarette could set this place goin' like a Roman Candle at New Year's," Huffmeister said , pulling a Zippo lighter out of his pocket and flicking it for effect.

The Prophet Ezekiel sputtered "But Huffmeister, this whole thing is just temporary, just for practice." Inspector Huffmeister snorted "temporary, shemporary, tell that to those hundreds of people stacked up like cord wood at the Copacabana fire way back then, tell them those poorly lit and blocked exits were just temporary." Huffmeister shouted the word "temporary" again and thrust his forefinger into the air. For a fleeting second the Inspector reminded him just a bit of one of his "wheezer" evangelists and he almost admired the fervor in his voice, but this thought passed quickly as The Prophet came back to his senses, realizing that the Inspector was not worried one lick about one single life, but only about an envelope.

Then The Prophet knew the only question he needed to ask, the only one that really mattered. He looked at the gloating pot bellied Inspector and said the magic words: "How much?" The Inspector rolled his eyes and said "The Prophet Ezekiel, I am going to be very nice to you because I admire you and what you are trying to do. Ya know I used to be interested in the ministry; in fact I was enrolled in a correspondence divinity school for two years—-The Northwestern California School of Divinity, based in Sacramento. Inspector rolled his eyes and said "The Prophet Ezekiel, I am going to very nice to you because I admire you and what you are trying to do. Yessir, I loved going to Divinity School and hated having to drop out because it was taking up so much of my time and was and negatively affecting my Building Inspector duties. But I still hold a great respect for "the calling," having been there myself, and that's why I like and admire your attempt at a career in evangelism. So it will be only five twenties; I will be right here waiting." And with that the Inspector grinned at The Prophet with his snaggly teeth and gazed with his pig eyes as The Prophet Ezekiel went into his trailer and into the cigar box in his closet where he had been saving up money for another sequined dress for Cinnamon and some hymnals and took out five twenties and put them in an envelope. He then returned to Inspector Huffmeister, who was busying himself thumbing through a North Carolina Building Code Manual that had been in his back pocket. When The Prophet handed him the money he quickly put the envelope inside his coat and only said "Guess you're okay now for a while The Prophet Ezekiel," and left the back yard. The Prophet was very upset and quietly shooed the remaining onlookers away telling them that he didn't feel well but they were welcome to return the next evening.

The Prophet Ezekiel was not one to brood and the next day found him full of vigor and ideas as he worked at his fence building job. After all he had already made a "prophecy", so he figgered that maybe he oughta work on the idea of a miracle. The Prophet thought he would proceed cautiously; then one day as he was reading the syndicated pharmacist column in the local newspaper he came across something that might be of use. The column was written by a husband and wife team named Zoe and Terry

Greeley, and The Prophet read it religiously. People wrote in with a question about pharmaceuticals and their particular effects in certain situations, and there were also lots of inquiries about the efficacy of home remedies, like things that would help gout or rubbing Vicks Vap-O-Rub on the bottoms of your feet and wearing socks to bed—-The Prophet had forgotten what exactly this particular treatment was supposed to cure, but he had seen it in the column a couple of times. Anyway, the question that caught his eye was the following: "Q—-Is there any treatment for Peyronie's disease? I am wondering about effectiveness and side effects".

Then the following response: "A—Peyronie's disease is a condition in which scar tissue has formed on the side of the penis. This leads it to bend during erection, a situation that may be painful." At this juncture The Prophet stopped reading and reflected a moment; he figgered most guys would give their left nut to have this affliction, but then thought that there must be more to the situation, like maybe it bent back at such an angle that you could never even get it in. The Prophet controlled his musings and continued to read the Greeley answer. "Doctors have tried quite a range of oral therapies for Peyronie's disease." When The Prophet Ezekiel read this he absolutely heehawed, until he realized by using the term "oral" the pharmacists were speaking of taking pills. "Could have been a great double entendre if they had meant it," he thought to himself as he continued to read. The pharmacists ended their answer by mentioning some sort of "injectable collagenase enzyme" which the thought of such a thing gave The Prophet a shiver. Apparently the Pharmacy Duet was not too hot on the idea either, mentioning about side effects including "bruising, swelling, and pain at the injection site." The Prophet chuckled at this, thinking that most guys would welcome the swelling.

This malady intrigued The Prophet in several different ways. For one he enjoyed the humor which he found in it, though realizing that the general populace would not find it as funny as he did. Another thing that grabbed him about it was the potential to somehow incorporate this condition into his nascent idea of performing a miracle, or a cure, if you will. And when word came that morning about ten o'clock that orange haired "Teener " Cline had been run over and killed the night before right on Killer 321 The Prophet Ezekiel knew it was time to get to the next step, the prophesy having come true. The Prophet figgered that "curing", or performing a miracle for someone afflicted with a situation such as "Peyronie's" had a couple of things going for it. The sexual aspect would lend itself to people not requiring a couple of things——first, a visual of the condition, and second, a visual of the cured individual. It seemed like the perfect deal; The Prophet makes a big commotion about some guy having this disease, The Prophet explains it delicately from the pulpit, then prays long and hard for the afflicted one, and a couple of weeks later The Prophet brings the Peyronie's victim back up and hears that he has been cured, many "Hosannas" and "Praise God"s to follow. "Who in the hell in a crowd is gonna want to see the 'before' or the 'after,'" The Prophet Ezekiel thought to himself. The Prophet decided it was a hell of an idea, and he knew who the "victim" would be.

After work that day The Prophet went home, cleaned up, and gathered Cinnamon and headed over to the Cline house to see and console the family of the dear departed "Teener." It was the typical scene of bereavement in the south when someone has died—-people coming and going, bringing casseroles and meat loafs and ham biscuits, and of course cakes and pies. This "comfort food" for the family was certainly in abundance in the little frame house nestled alongside Highway 321, and there was quite a crowd in attendance, seeing the family and offering their condolences or generally milling about, inside and outside in the yard. The Prophet Ezekiel and Cinnamon threaded their way through the group until they reached the living room, where the family was ensconsed. Word had spread about the "prophesy" that had come true, and many of the attendees present looked upon The Prophet with awe filled eyes The Prophet saw this, but did not acknowledge, choosing to work his way to the side of the grief stricken parents. Gladys and Theodore Cline, parents of the deceased, were sitting beside each other on a ratty sofa with plastic covers over it. As The Prophet looked at this he thought that maybe the Clines had instituted the covering a little late, but suppressed the desire to emit a chuckle. Instead he confronted Glades and Theodore, or "Mutt" and "Coconut," as they were known in the neighborhood.

Mutt was a tall heavy set woman who worked third shift at the Mariposa spinning mill in South Gastonia. Coconut loafed around and did an odd job once in a while. His unusual nickname came from his appearance, more specifically his head. He had thinning brown hair and near the top of his forehead were two moles about three inches apart and a little smaller than a dime in size. As The Prophet Ezekiel looked at Mr. Cline it sent him back in time to when his mother would send him out onto the back porch with a coconut, a hammer, a 16 penny nail, a knife, a bowl, and a glass. He would drive the nail into the two dark indentions in the coconut, which closely resembled Mr. Cline's moles, and drain the milk into the glass. Then he would lay the coconut on the concrete floor and tap on it with the hammer until it cracked in several places. The next task was to separate the white coconut meat from the shell. The outside of the shell had a light wispy hair like covering, not a lot different in appearance to Mr. Cline's head. Thus the appellation.

As The Prophet approached Mrs. Cline she first grinned at him, showing small snuff stained teeth, and then burst into tears. "Oh my, it is so nice of you to come here; I hear you are going to be an evangelist, and that you prophesied that someone would die on the highway," Mrs. Cline said, tears streaming down her sallow cheeks and a little drab of snuff spit making its way out of the left side of her mouth.

"That is true, Mrs. Cline, and I have legally changed my name to The Prophet Ezekiel in preparation for this new career, which I will launch soon. And it is also true that I did prophesy that a life would be lost along Highway 321. Of course I had no idea that it would be your dear daughter Tina; if I had had any inkling I surely would have warned you all." The Prophet was displaying what he liked to call his "omniscient and understanding" smile; it was one he had been working on a lot and he felt like he had it down purty good. He felt even better about his performance when Mrs. Cline launched into an ear shattering wailing, giving The Prophet the opportunity to console her. The Prophet hugged Mrs. Cline and she kissed him on the cheek, depositing a small blob of snuff spittle there. Cinnamon quickly pulled a tissue from her purse and cleaned up The Prophet; then it was time to see to Mr. Cline.

"It's just been awawawawawaaawwwwful," Mr. Cline offered. In addition to having a head that closely resembled a coconut he had been afflicted all his life with a severe stuttering problem.

"I know, Mr. Cline, I know," The Prophet said, "but it is not for us to know why things turn out the way they do, it is only for us to seek the answer and PRAY FOR FORGIVENESS." As The Prophet virtually bellowed these last three words the twenty or so people around hushed , exactly the reaction The Prophet desired. At that point The Prophet placed his left hand on Mutt's frizzy grey hair and his right on the thin hair of Coconut, just above the moles, and said "Would everyone please bow their heads in prayer?" As one the group bowed their heads and closed their eyes and The Prophet lit into it.

"Dear Lord, " he began, "we are gathered here this evening to remember our dear departed friend, daughter, sister, and to honor her for the righteous life she led, and to pray for her soul, for we know she is up in heaven this very moment." Here several "Praise Gods" and "Amens" were shouted out, and Mutt started wailing a little bit. The Prophet continued. "And Most Holy and Exalted Father, we beseech thee to comfort Tina's family, and all of her friends who have gathered here to honor her." More "Amens" and a smattering of "hallelujahs" erupted and The Prophet Ezekiel paused for a moment to respond with "Amen Brothers and Sisters."

Then he raised his eyes and looked around, knowing full well that most of the people there had already raised theirs and were looking at him. The Prophet had sensed that they would be; he then launched into his climax.

"In closing, our dear Lord, Heavenly Father of our Savior Jesus Christ, we pray for you to help us through these difficult times, and we pray that we may grow in your spirit and wisdom. In Jesus' name, Amen."

When The Prophet Ezekiel said "Amen" a chorus of amens accompanied him and as he looked at Mutt and Coconut's tear stained upturned faces he smiled beatifically and hugged them, one arm around each neck.

As their embrace with The Prophet Ezekiel came to a close Mutt and Coconut looked at each other and whispered very quietly for a few seconds and then Mutt grabbed the hands of The Prophet and said "we want you to preach Teener's funeral; can you see it in your heart to honor us so?" The Prophet Ezekiel was a bit shocked but was able to conceal it, his cool demeanor being from a lot of lessons learned in street fighting and various fracases in which he had been involved. The Prophet had always noticed that the "cool guys", the ones who could maintain, were the ones who won the day; utilizing that wisdom he again gave his most beatific smile and said, so very graciously, "Of course I will, you all just let me know where and when," and with that a very buoyant The Prophet Ezekiel made his departure; he needed to talk to the dear departed's older brother Willie.

The Prophet found Willie Cline in the kitchen, where he had just loaded up a plate with banana pudding, a piece of coconut cake, a fourth of an apple pie, and three Krispy Kreme donuts. "Hey Willie," The Prophet said, standing by where the hungry boy was seated at the kitchen table. The table had chrome double legs and chrome around the sides; the top was a mingled yellow formica with a section in the middle that could be pulled out.

"Hey Willie," said The Prophet softly, smiling at the gangly gap toothed brother of the deceased. Willie Cline was about 6' 2", slender, stooped, and had greasy dirty blonde hair that was always a little long and shaggy; his I. Q. had revealed a score of 85. He gave The Prophet Ezekiel a goofy smile as he looked at him. "Sorry 'bout your sister, " The Prophet said as Willie ladled cake and banana pudding into his mouth. Willie had a very bad case of acne, which would probably get quite a bit worse considering the sugar he was consuming. Willie gave The Prophet his customary goofy grin and holding up a tablespoonful of banana pudding said "Good shit , ain't it?"

The Prophet Ezekiel leaned down close to Willie Cline and said "How about I give you a chance to be the center of attention and earn ten dollars on top of that?" Willie looked up quickly and between gulps of dessert managed to get out a muffled "Sure Zeke". The Prophet quickly told him how he should be addressed from that day forward; "The Prophet Ezekiel is now my legal name and that's what you need to call me," The Prophet said. Willie Cline started laughing and almost choked on his coconut cake but managed to get out "you ain't no damn prophet Zeke——what you comin' on with that shit about anyway?" The Prophet was starting to get annoyed; Willie was beginning to test his evangelical patience. The Prophet leaned over closer and whispered into Willie Cline's waxy blackhead laden ear "Lissen asshole, you wanta be on stage and get ten bucks or not; I can always get somebody else." This got Willie's attention and he quickly agreed that he did want the money and his moment in the limelight, so The Prophet suggested they go out on the back porch and discuss the details.

As they stepped outside The Prophet offered Willie Cline one of his Marlboro cigarettes, which he greedily grabbed. "Hey, The Prophet Ezekiel, you ain't got no dope on ya have ya?" Willie asked. "I don't do that shit no more you dumbass and don't ever mention it around me any more,"The Prophet said. Willie Cline hung his head and replied "Okay, The Prophet Ezekiel." The Prophet then explained to Willie what he had to do to get the money and the fame. Without getting too technical The Prophet explained the Peyronie's situation that he was supposed to be afflicted with and told him that all he would have to do would be to dress nice, or the best he could, and just stand up at the meeting as The Prophet told the group what was going on and how The Prophet Ezekiel was for his first miracle going to pray non-stop until Willie Cline was cured.

"Now Willie, this problem is supposed to affect your pecker purty drastically, so I want you to stand kinda funny when I introduce you, kinda like you are favoring one side, and maybe even sorta put your hand near your crotch almost like you are gonna grab it, like the black boys do all the time." "You mean like this?", asked Willie, as he grabbed his pecker and squeezed it.

"Well, more like you are gettin' ready to do it, instead of actually doin' it", replied The Prophet. Then The Prophet Ezekiel told Willie Cline about how he would appear again just one week later and stand straight and tall and smiling as The Prophet Ezekiel told everybody 'bout how Willie had been miraculously cured. "And they'll believe it?" Willie asked dubiously.

"Sure they will, 'cause I , The Prophet Ezekiel will be tellin' the story. Trust me Willie; you'll be famous. It might even get ya some 'tang," The Prophet said, smiling broadly as Willie Cline giggled. "Ya think I could show 'em my trick?" Willie cline asked. The Prophet immediately knew what Willie was talkin' about; Willie did not have a whole lot going for him on any level or any strata of humanity, but he did have one talent that he could perform. Willie Cline could pick his nose with his tongue. Virtually everyone knew about this because Willie had done it for years if anybody brought it up. The Prophet himself had seen Willie do it many times; in fact, when he was still known as Zeke Taylor The Prophet used to go through a big production of introducing Willie Cline whenever there was a bunch of guys around. Zeke would always do it the same way; "Ladies and Gentlemen, it is my great honor to introduce to you a man who can do something that no other human being can even attempt, a local man who has grown up here in our community and has occasionally attended our local schools, and is rumored to have gone to that Baptist Church that Morris Hight's daddy preached at, there on Highway 321, at least once, but whose one outstanding God Given talent will be displayed at this time. " Then the guy known as Zeke Taylor would pause for about ten seconds, for effect, and say "I give to you Willie Cline and his famous tongue up his nose booger pickin' trick."

Whatever bunch was present would clap and holler and sometimes chant "Will-eee, Will-eee," until Willie Cline stood front and center. Then the show would begin in earnest. First Willie would stick his tongue out and quickly flick the end of his nose; agreed that this preliminary trick was aided by the curved hawkish honker he had, but the act always incited the onlookers to try to touch their nose with their tongue ,always unsuccessfully. Willie would then move his tongue all over the end of his nose; anyone who observed Willie Cline always came away talking about how long and thin his tongue was, not at all thick like a human tongue, but more narrow and thin like one would imagine a rat's tongue to be. So after teasing the crowd for a while Willie would insert his tongue into his right nostril, and then his left, repeatedly, pushing his rat tongue inside each nose hole a good inch and a half. This usually brought quite a varied reaction from the onlookers, from cheers to "oh gross" to just walking away in disgust.

So when Willie Cline inquired about "doin' his trick" at church The Prophet Ezekiel immediately shouted a resounding "no" and assured Willie that the ten dollars he was going to get would never, ever, be paid if he did it. Willie Cline sheepishly agreed to the terms, mumbling "I was just kiddin, The Prophet Ezekiel" and trundled back into the kitchen to devour more acne inspiring desserts.

The Prophet stood silently on the little porch and reflected on where he was; he was going to preach his first funeral. The Prophet smiled a beatific smile, a truly real one, collected his lovely Cinnamon and headed back to his trailer.

"Teener" Cline's funeral wasn't until Saturday afternoon so The Prophet had a couple days to get prepared. The funeral was going to be at The Plainview Baptist Church just down the road, set back in a grove of pecan trees right off Killer 321 highway. The church was pastored by a mill worker who had been called to the ministry a few years back, Fred Hight. Pastor Hight was known for two things; his mild mannered demeanor in everyday life, and his fiery hell fire and brimstone sermons he delivered every Sunday. Pastor Hight was a widower, and his late wife had left him with two young children when she had passed away nine years before, a boy and a girl who were only a year apart in age. The boy, Morris, maybe because he was mad about his momma dying or maybe because he was being the typical bad, bad, preacher's son was way more than Pastor Hight could handle. Morris delighted in laying drunk frequently and it was a given he would always attend church every Sunday and always be sloppy drunk. The girl, Lynnette, was 16, one year younger then Morris and every bit as wild as Morris in her own way. Her acts of rebellion included screwing 'bout every boy in the senior class at Ranlo High School and wearing very, very short skirts with no panties.

When the grief stricken Clines had approached Pastor Hight with their idea of having The Prophet Ezekiel preach "Teener's" funeral he understood totally, what with The Prophet sort of having prophesied Teener's demise, and told them immediately that it would be no problem for him, but that they would have to take it up with the Chief Deacon of the Plainview Baptist Church, Mr. William Hall. Deacon Bill, as he was known locally, had worked all his life at Firestone mill in Gastonia and was very robust; he also tended a very productive two acre garden in his back yard. When the Clines heard what they needed to do they just walked down the gravel drive behind their house to the Hall home, for the Halls had been long time neighbors in the community. The Clines and the Halls did not know each other very well; although the Clines were technically members at Plainview they rarely attended.

    Gladys and Theodore Cline were walking up the gravel drive to the home of Deacon Bill Hall and his wife Relemina. The driveway was pretty long and curved around a couple of times before arriving at the brick veneer house with a carport on the right side. The Clines knew the Halls were at home, for hey had espied Deacon Bill's red Ford in the driveway. Relemina,, who was darkly complected and rumored to be of French descent from Charleston, South Carolina, did not work "public work", spending her time housekeeping and tending to the yard and canning and freezing vegetables from Deacon Bill's big garden. The Clines did notice that the Halls' boy, Raeford, was there, as his little grey Volkswagen bug was parked off to the right side of the carport, that spot being reserved for the red Ford. They walked up into the carport and knocked on the door and in a few seconds Raeford Hall opened the door; Raeford grinned at them as he was munching on a barbecued chicken leg, the sauce liberally coating his lips. Raeford was a trim fellow, about 5'9" tall and 150 pounds. He was a senior and a good track man at Ranlo High School, where he was on the annual staff; additionally, he contributed occasionally to the local newspaper, sports writing being his forte. "Why hello, Mr. and Mrs. Cline, won't you come in," Raeford Hall said. Gladys and Theodore both thought 'bout how polite and nice Raeford was; of course, if they had been aware of how many times he had screwed their dear departed daughter in the Hall living room when his parents went to the beach each summer they would have been whistling a very different tune. This scenario passed through

Raeford's mind as he ushered the Clines out of the kitchen and into the living room where Bill and Relemina were sitting on the sofa relaxing, the very venue where their son and the late "Teener" had had their fun.

"Look who is here, folks," Raeford called to his parents, resuming his attack on the chicken leg. Deacon Bill and Relemina both stood up and embraced Gladys and Theodore Cline, which spawned some "water works" from Gladys and a profound aura of sadness from Theodore. "We are so sorry for your loss; we know the pain must be unbearable," Deacon Bill pronounced, utilizing a low comforting tone of voice which he usually reserved for Official Board meetings. "Is there anything at all we can do for you?" At this point Relemina Hall embraced Gladys once again, the motion fomenting another loud sob from Mrs. Cline and a "for real " tear traveling down the right side of Relemina's face; the drop left a little track in Mrs. Hall's makeup.

After a moment Coconut composed himself enough to get down to business. "Well Deacon Hall, we wanted to ask a favor of you. We know you are the head of the Official Board of Plainview Baptist and we want to have our baby "Teener's" funeral there this Saturday. The Deacon adopted his most thoughtful pose and said "Why Theodore, seeing as how you all are members in good standing I see no impediment to your having the funeral there. Why would you even ask the question?" Deacon Bill asked.

Theodore Cline looked a little sheepish as he said, "Well Deacon Hall, we want to bring in a different preacher to officiate; now of course we have already talked to Pastor Fred Hight about this and that is why we are here; Pastor Hight said the final approval would be up to you." Deacon Bill crossed his muscular wiry arms and smiled at Theodore Cline. "Of course that will be fine, Mr. Cline; by the way, who is the guest minister?".

"The Prophet Ezekiel," answered Coconut. "He is a family friend and is sort of an evangelist in training."

Deacon Bill shook his head and said "I don't rightly know that name".

"Well he used to be known as Zeke Taylor, but he went before Judge Bulwinkle and got his name changed all legal and proper and I swear he prayed the sweetest prayer I ever heard over at our house last night," said Coconut.

Deacon Bill nodded. "Of course, I know him; and you have my blessing——we will be in attendance at the funeral." At that the Clines departed, and both of them noticed that Raeford Hall had looked so dewy eyed and sad as he closed the kitchen door behind them.

"He is an awfully sweet and sentimental boy," said Gladys, as Coconut nodded tearfully. Inside the kitchen door Raeford Hall wiped away the moisture from his face, and brightened up as he realized he had several months before his parents' annual beach trip to recruit "Teener's" replacement.

It was Saturday morning, 10:00 a.m. and The Prophet Ezekiel was reviewing his notes on what was going to happen at Teener Cline's funeral, which was slated for 2:00 p. m. at Plainview Baptist Church. The Clines had told him that all was well with the Official Board as far as The Prophet preaching the funeral. He had not expected any problem from Deacon Bill Hall, and had even solidified the situation by posing a question to the Deacon—would the Deacon consider asking his son, Raeford, the leader of the Royal Ambassadors, the young men's group in the Baptist denomination, if Raeford could gather some of the RAs, as they were called, to act as a sort of color guard during the half hour of viewing the body prior to the funeral. The Prophet Ezekiel explained to the Deacon that although the RAs did not have uniforms, if they all wore black slacks, short sleeved white shirts, and simple black ties that it would all look very official. The Prophet suggested that there be four of them, two standing behind the casket and one at each end. Deacon Bill Hall quickly agreed to this and assured The Prophet Ezekiel that he and his "boy" would take care of it. Deacon Bill was satisfied this would not be a problem, for although he and his seventeen year old son did not always see eye to eye, the "boy" owed him one big time.

The Deacon had rescued his wild ass twice in the last six months; the first episode was when Raeford and his best friend Dean Norman got drunk and ran away in Norman's old pick up truck, the idea being to move to Charleston, South Carolina and work on a fishing boat. When they sobered up a little and ran out of money and gas in Columbia the Deacon had wired them thirty dollars to get them back home. But the biggest deal Raeford had pulled was only two months previously when Raeford and his crazy "girl friend of the month", a hot little thing named Cassandra Davis, whose old man had a welding business on the Lower Dallas Road, decided to run off and get married. When THEY sobered up and found out her parents would have to sign for her the Deacon and Relemina had actually driven to Clover, South Carolina and escorted them back, the Deacon driving Raeford's old Toyota with the kids in the back and Relemina driving the family car. Deacon Bill Hall gave the kids "almighty hell" on the way back; he thought he actually approached the intensity of some of Pastor Fred Hight's wild sermons at Plainview. So when Deacon Bill Hall brought the subject up to his "boy" Raeford he immediately agreed and promised that he and three RAs he would recruit would be on site at 1:30 p.m. at the moment Tenner Cline's casket would be opened for viewing.

Raeford Hall knew right away who he could count on for the "color guard"; he quickly called Danny Motes, who lived down the road near Bill's Food Center, Kenny Harris, whose dad owned Bill's Food Center, and Calvin Cooley, a bully who lived across the road from Raeford. He included Calvin Cooley in the group because he knew if he didn't there would hell to pay and Raeford would more than likely get his ass whipped. After the phone calls Raeford reflected on things and figgered that he had done a purty good job; he thought it especially appropriate that Kenny Harris be included 'cause poor Teener Cline had been squashed right in front of Bill's Food Center, of course standing on the edge of the shoulder like always. Raeford felt like he had done a good job so he put the funeral out of his mind for the moment; he had more important things to attend to, like seeing how many Country Club Malt Liquors he could drink that Friday night at the Meadowbrook Supper Club.

It was high noon the day of the funeral and The Prophet Ezekiel was having a little trouble getting started on what he was gonna say at Teener Cline's funeral. The first thing he thought of was recounting all the positive things in Teener's life, but coming up with positives about Teener exhausted even the fertile and creative mind of The Prophet Ezekiel. The Prophet had read that it was helpful to chat informally with the bereaved family to get ideas, things like sweet memories or little meaningful interchanges between the dear departed and her loved ones, but after spending an hour with Mutt and Coconut just that morning The Prophet felt a bit nonplussed. For example, when he had asked Mutt Cline what she was most proud of Teener for she had pondered for a moment and replied, "Well, she got out of the ninth grade after only two years; it took Willie three." The Prophet had then looked at Coconut, who was nodding and smiling broadly. When The Prophet had asked if there was anything else they could think of and Mutt said, "and she never got pregnant, not even once." This comment set Coconut to nodding and smiling once again and made The Prophet think it might be time to go, but as he was rising to leave Coconut's eyes lit up and he said, "and I never saw her pick her nose with her tongue, never even saw her make the attempt——-but I'm sure she coulda done it if she had really wanted to." Coconut then nodded and smiled at The Prophet Ezekiel and The Prophet thanked the Clines effusively and departed.

When The Prophet Ezekiel got home to the single wide he went right away into his little study and took out his King James Version Bible he had received when he had been promoted to the Primary Class in church and started reading the New Testament. The Prophet had decided that he was pretty much a New Testament man; he felt like it would make him come across a little more progressive than the average pastor, for example, Pastor Fred Hight, in whose church The Prophet was going to preach Teener Cline's funeral, his very first. As he opened the New Testament he read on the first page: THE NEW TESTAMENT of our Lord and Saviour Jesus Christ, translated out of the original Greek." The Prophet had never known a Greek but of course had read about them and their place in history; in fact,one of his favorite jokes prior to his decision to be an evangelist was to start up a conversation about famous Greeks, mention some names like Demosthenes, Socrates, Herodotus, and Plato and then announce "and of course the most famous Greek was the philosopher Testicles." He always got a good response for this one, for the typical group he was in front of had no idea who those other Greeks were, but they had heard of testicles. The Prophet chuckled a little as he started into reading "The Gospel According to St. Matthew". As The Prophet lit into chapter one he got tired real quick of all the "begetting", but hung in there, and he felt like it got more interesting after Jesus was born and they got going on ol' King Herod and The Three Wise Men and such. The Prophet thought it odd how Matthew apparently got into warp speed and took Jesus from a baby to a grown man in going from Chapter 2 to 3. And The Prophet was purty interested there in Chapter 4; there was a bunch going on in there, what with the Devil tempting Jesus and Jesus startin' to preach and all. The Prophet also liked the story 'bout Jesus seeing Simon Peter and his brother Andrew casting a net into the sea and Jesus telling them to "Follow me, and I will make you fishers of men." This struck a chord with The Prophet; he remembered when they learned a little song about that one time in Vacation Bible School: "I will make you fishers of men, fishers of men, fishers of men. I will make you fishers of men if you follow me. If you follow me, if you follow me. I will make you fishers of men if you follow me." The Prophet chuckled a bit thinking of this little song; it took him way back to sky blue days when there were no problems and you went to Vacation Bible School every summer and made all those neat posters and things and on Friday night all the parents came and "looked and aaaaahhhhed" over all the stuff their particular lil punkin had accomplished. And then they would all have supper in the Educational Building, topped off by multiple flavors of homemade ice cream.

Then The Prophet Ezekiel read Chapter 4, verse 24, and it seemed like it just fit into his plan to be an evangelist: "And His fame went throughout all Syria and they brought unto him all sick people that were taken with divers diseases and torments, and those were possessed with devils, and those which were lunatic and those that had the palsy; and he healed them." The Prophet thought about the time he had seen a woman with palsy; everybody called it the "shakin'" palsy. The occasion had been the graduation ceremony from Costner Elementary School when his sister Gail had finished the eighth grade. There was a rather plain, homely girl in her class named Faye Coxey; Faye and her brother Ray and her parents lived down the road from the Taylors in a shotgun rental house. The Prophet remembered that he had seen Mr. Coxey; he was a tall angular man who dressed in old suits, always wore a hat and had big yellow teeth. Mr. Coxey drove an ancient car; it seemed like his clothes and automobile matched in that they both looked about thirty years old. There was a rumor that Mr. Coxey had been a successful salesman until something bad had happened.

But he had never seen Mrs. Coxey, and once he saw her he would never forget her. The graduation program was about to begin when Mr. Coxey came into the auditorium escorting his wife. The daughter, Faye, immediately rushed from her seat, grinning widely. The Prophet recalled that Faye Coxey had short, straight chopped off hair and that she was wearing bright red lipstick. It was the same color that her mother was wearing on her face—-literally. Apparently Mr. Coxey had allowed his wife to apply her own lipstick and it was all over her face, but admittedly a good portion did wind up on her mouth. The poor woman was all aquiver, Mr. Coxey assisting her along and smiling, showing his giant yellow teeth. The Prophet remembered the look of joy and pride on the young Coxey girl's face as she rushed to meet her mother and father and help them get seated. She sat on the stage and beamed at her mother during the entire program and the kind and courteous country folk gathered in the Costner Elementary School graciously did not stare at the poor woman; if they had they would have seen a woman of about fifty swaddled in an old beaver coat that was losing pretty large patches of fur, a woman who shook at times mildly and at other times more violently, her yellow toothed husband holding her tightly all the while.

The Prophet Ezekiel then continued into the Fifth Chapter of Matthew and it was there that his blue eyes lit up, and there that he beamed a broad smile; it there that he found the inspiration for his sermon for Teener Cline's funeral.

Raeford had told the Royal Ambassadors to meet at the little vestibule at the entry to Plainview Baptist Church; the vestibule served as the location where whoever was handing out bulletins would be stationed and where prior to the service one of the church fathers would pull on the rope which ascended through the ceiling to the church bell, alerting everyone that it was time for the show to be begin. Raeford looked at the worn rope and remembered how his Deacon Daddy had let him ring the bell on many occasions. Of course the bell would not be ringing today, what with the somber occasion of Teener Cline's funeral and all. The three Royal Ambassador invitees were in attendance; Danny Motes and Kenny Harris were dressed exactly like Raeford had suggested, and Calvin Cooley had done 'bout as good as he could, though his white shirt could have been cleaner. The Cooley family was not known for its excessive hygiene; most of the neighborhood women blamed it on the abrupt departure of Elvin Cooley after a steamy liaison with a midget from the county fair last fall. If you wanted your ass beat right quick just mention the words "dwarf" or "midget around ol' Calvin Cooley. Raeford Hall ignored the slovenly bully and went over the pertinent facts, where they would be stationed in relation to the casket, where they would be seated in the front row when Blair Houser of The Dallas Funeral Home and his boys would wheel ol' Teener's casket in, and how the Royal Ambassador Color Guard was not to assume their positions until the funeral director had opened the lid of the casket. It was precisely 1:25 when the long black Cadillac hearse pulled into the gravel parking lot of Plainview Baptist Church and Blair falls and three of his nattily dressed associates emerged from the vehicle. Blair opened the rear of the hearse and pulled out Teener's casket, the spring loaded cart under the casket jumping into place, and they proceeded to roll Teener in the front door of Plainview. Earlier they had placed a large spray of gladiolus at each end of where the casket would rest; the four of them pushed the box to the proper location between the flower stands, and then sticking strictly to the funeral script the handsome silver haired funeral director opened the end lid of Teener Cline's casket and turned to the audience and nodded to where Raeford Hall and the Royal ambassador Color guard sat on the front row, ready to spring into action. When Blair Falls nodded to Raeford he also smiled, flashing his beautiful false teeth recently purchased in Anderson, South Carolina at The Tooth Emporium, one of those places where they pulled your teeth and fitted you with a full set of dentures all on the same day. There was a big color billboard on Interstate 85 at the Anderson exit extolling the virtues of The Tooth Emporium; it showed three septuagenarians' faces side by side, their jaws and cheeks slack with the absence of teeth, and next to it the same three smiling broadly with a new set of choppers. Raeford Hall was heartened to see Blair's new teeth, for what with the newness of the dentures and everything Blair had forgotten to insert them a couple of times before he left home. But he had 'em in today and was lookin' good; most women thought Blair Falls handsome and he had a reputation of being a ladies' man.

So on cue Raeford, Danny, Kenny, and Calvin walked to the now opened casket, their heads slightly downcast in respect to the late Teener Cline, and assumed their positions. They all followed the plan Raeford had given them perfectly: Calvin at the head of the casket, Kenny at the foot, and Raeford and Danny standing behind. Raeford had wanted things to look very professional, what with him being head of the Royal Ambassadors and all, and it came off perfectly. Just as Raeford had told them to do, the four Royal Ambassadors assumed their positions, holding the downcast, solemn look , and then, as one, quickly raised their heads and assumed a sort of military parade rest pose. They got it purty good; at least it was probably the most organized endeavor that had ever been carried out at a funeral at Plainview Baptist Church. At that point Blair Falls Houser, the funeral director, who had remained standing a short distance away, motioned to the funeral attendees that it was time to parade by the casket to show their final tribute to the dear departed Teener Cline. The crowd came row by row, kinda like parishioners do at Communion, and the first group was walking by and stopping and looking at Teener———-one of her aunts even smiled down at her and pinched her dead chubby cheek——- when a guy came racing, or rather staggering, up the main aisle and positioned himself right beside Calvin Cooley at the head of the casket. The boy was dressed in a madres short sleeved shirt and white Bermuda shorts and was wearing flip flops. He sort of rolled to a stop there and just stood grinning a goofy grin at the crowd; it was Morris Hight, and he was being true to the form he assumed every time he darkened the door of his daddy's church, which was being shit faced, knee walking drunk, having already killed one of two half pints of Popov Vodka he had bought that morning down at Mr. Moose's double wide trailer. Raeford Hall was aghast; Morris Hight had called him the day before going on about how since his daddy was the resident preacher he should be allowed to be in the Royal Ambassador Color Guard. Raeford had very calmly and logically explained to Morris, who was drunk when he called Raeford, that the Color Guard had already been chosen; Raeford exhibited great reserve in dealing with Morris Hight, especially since Morris was not even a member of the Royal Ambassadors, and had even egged them in a meeting room during one of their weekly gatherings, bursting in the door, throwing eggs, and scampering around like Ernest T. Bass did on that episode of Andy Griffith where Barney and Andy attempted to "civilize" the mountain boy and they all went to the party at the Mayberry "high society" lady's house and Ernest T. Bass uttered his most famous greeting——"How do you do Mrs. Wiley", and met Rowmena, and Mrs. Wiley thought he was from backbay Boston, and then it all fell apart and Ernest T. and Rowmena started leap frogging over bushes.

Raeford Hall could not believe his eyes, but yet he could; Morris and his sister Leeanne seemed to try to do anything and everything in their power to embarrass their minister father, who was sitting quietly near the front of the church and at that very moment shaking his head sadly as he watched the antics of his only son. Then as if it had been choreographed Leeanne Hight, who was seated at her customary spot on the back row, gave out a cackle and pointed at her brother. Leeanne was also ripped, having killed a half pint of Bourbon De Luxe and smoked half a joint with her boyfriend Harry McAbee, who was sitting beside her. Leeanne had on a skirt that struck her at mid-thigh when she was standing; she was pantiless, Harry's hand being out of sight far up the skirt. Raeford knew there was nothing to do but tough it out and try to maintain decorum with the Royal Ambassador Color Guard unit. Everyone was being okay with the exception of Calvin Cooley, who had hollered and waved at Leeanne Hight when she had giggled. Of course Morris Hight had to "cut a shine" as the old phrase went; the first thing he did was walk around and bend down and kiss ol' Teener on her forehead, blubbering "no more quarter stuff", referring to the very credible rumor that that was what could get you some "affection" from the departed. All of the Color Guard had heard this; in fact every last one of them had participated in the exchange, but they managed to keep a straight face. Mercifully, Morris went back to his previous spot and by the time the thirty minute viewing period was getting close to being over Morris had tired out a little, sitting cross-legged at the head of Teener's casket next to Calvin Cooley, and then had just fallen over on his side and begun snoring loudly. Blair Falls Houser, standing at his post nearby, walked over and tenderly picked up the pickled wannabe Royal Ambassador and carried him out the side door of the church. Then, as it was two o'clock and the viewing period was over Blair falls walked over and closed the casket lid over Teener Cline. On cue, as orchestrated by the funeral director, The Prophet Ezekiel entered from the rear of the church and walked to the communion rail where Teener Cline's casket lay. At this moment Blair Houser nodded lightly to Raeford Hall and the Royal Ambassador Color Guard, minus the already departed uninvited Morris Hight, took their seats. The Prophet looked over to Frances Hayes, the long time organist at Plainview Baptist Church and raised his right hand slightly and she began a soft rendition of "Just As I Am". Then the double doors leading in from the vestibule where the church bell was were opened wide, each door held by one of Blair Falls Houser's associates, and Teener's family entered. Gladys and Theodore led the family in to the church, Gladys having the assistance of a strong arm of one of Blair's boys on her right side. Behind Mutt and Coconut Willie Cline walked, cleaned up about as well as could be expected. He had his usual goofy-ass look on his face and once in a while would flick his rat-like tongue out. After Willie there was an entourage of aunts and uncles and cousins who followed Mutt and Coconut. They were all seated on the first two pews on the right hand side of the church.

Everyone was standing in respect for Teener's family, for after The Prophet had motioned to the organist he had slowly and solemnly lifted his upturned palms waist high. Blair Falls and Associates got everybody seated and after Blair had nodded to The Prophet the former Zeke Taylor lowered his hands and all took their seats. The Prophet Ezekiel then addressed the flock.

Using his best wry smile of resignation and acceptance The Prophet Ezekiel said "Please let us pray: Dear Omniscient and Omnipotent God in Heaven, we beseech ye to bless this gathering congregated here today to honor the life of Teener Cline, a child who has been tragically taken from us. We will miss her sweet smile and we reflect upon her life as one ended too soon but one she spent thinking of others first, over herself, especially her parents, Gladys and Theodore, solid citizens of our community and proud parents of Teener." At this point Gladys, who had been sniffling quietly, let out a plaintive wail and just kept on getting, it for a good ten seconds, followed by hollers of "Oh my poor baby, oh my precious lil redhead." The Prophet slowly walked the five feet to the first pew, and smiling his best consoling smile leaned over and put his arms around Gladys Cline. Almost immediately she was comforted and within twenty seconds The Prophet was able to pull away and resume his former position, and it was not a second too soon because the mixed aroma of Railroad Mills snuff and way too much Gardenia perfume had just about stifled him.

The Prophet Ezekiel returned to the front to face the crowd and spoke. "I am The Prophet Ezekiel," he said, watching the group very closely as he spoke these words, thinking that maybe there might be some smirks, but everyone looked attentive and tuned in to his speech as he went on to explain how he had come to be the officiating pastor and how gracious Rev. Fred Hight and Deacon William Hall had been in allowing him to be there today. The Prophet then proceeded; "I am going to read from Ezekiel 3:12," he said, moving to behind the lectern and picking up his Bible. "Then the spirit took me up, and I heard behind me a voice of a great rushing, saying BLESSED be the Glory of the Lord from his place." The Prophet Ezekiel paused to look at the audience, gauging them, before he raised his voice almost to a shout and repeated the last part of the scripture; "blessed be the glory of the Lord from his place." At the end of this sentence The Prophet definitely had EVERYONE'S attention, and he looked at them solemnly.

The Prophet then took his planned fifteen second pause, and allowed a light smile to appear on his face. "Brothers and Sisters in Christ," he said, "in times such as these it is very difficult to feel 'blessed', like I just read about in the Scripture. But I want all of you to relax a moment and reflect on how 'blessed' we are. Oh yes, we are gathered here to honor and grieve for Teener Cline, a sweet and joyful girl who has been ripped from our lives by a horrible accident, but we need to expand our thinking and emotions beyond this very sad moment, this very, very sad moment when we pay tribute to and say goodbye to Teener Cline. I beseech you to think of the times when you were with Teener and passed the time of day with her in joy and in love." The Prophet paused a moment as Raeford Hall fidgeted and coughed, looking more than a bit uncomfortable, no doubt memories of a quarter's worth of Teener's "joy" wafting through his mind. The Prophet smiled reassuringly at Raeford and continued. " I want everyone to think about a joyful moment with Teener, and I want everyone to think about it silently, and I want you to do it for a full minute, beginning now."

The Prophet Ezekiel then began walking around, up and down the narrow aisles of Plainview Baptist Church, catching the eye of many of the group, and when he did smiling his beatific smile and giving his reassuring nod. After a while he walked back up to the lectern and resumed.

"Yes, today I am speaking of being blessed, and particularly of how blessed we all were to have known Teener Cline. But when we truly think about being blessed, even at this time of immeasurable sorrow, I think we should gain perspective and should in this moment of honoring our dear departed Teener make mention of the words of Jesus, from The Sermon On The Mount, from St. Matthew chapter 5, verses 1-11: 'And seeing the multitudes, he went up into a mountain: and when he was set, his disciples came unto him; and he opened his mouth and taught them, saying Blessed are the poor in spirit: for theirs is the Kingdom of Heaven. Blessed are they that mourn: for they shall be comforted". The Prophet stopped for a moment and walked over to Gladys and Theodore and said "Remember this passage, my children, Matthew, Chapter 5, verse 4, and remember it well, and let it comfort you: Blessed are they that mourn, for they shall be comforted". The Prophet looked at them unsmiling, but displaying his most earnest look, and walked back to the lectern, but not before letting his eyes scan the crowd, now a very "into the moment" crowd.

When The Prophet got back behind the lectern and looked at Gladys and Theodore he could see that their sniveling, whiney, crying demeanor had been replaced by a calmness, maybe even a look of hope. As The Prophet Ezekiel quickly assessed the group again he thought he saw some other similar looks——-"I believe I got 'em thinkin' a little,"he said to himself.

The Prophet Ezekiel continued. "Blessed are the meek; for they shall inherit the earth. Blessed are they which do hunger and thirst after righteousness; for they shall be filled. Blessed are the merciful; for they shall obtain mercy. Blessed are the pure in heart; for they shall see God." He stopped and walked away from the lectern to stand in front of the Cline family. He then repeated Matthew, Chapter 5, verse 8; "Blessed are the pure in heart; for they shall see God," and then as he stood there in front of the Clines he smiled his most beautiful smile and said "Gladys, Theodore, Willie, all of us know that Teener was pure in heart, and therefore all of us are satisfied that Teener in this very moment is seeing God. Although her corporeal body is still with us, we know that her soul has gone on to be with Jesus Christ our Heavenly Father." The Prophet got resigned smiles from the Cline parents after this speech; when he glanced at their son Willie grinned at him and flicked his rat tongue up to touch the end of his nose. The Prophet then read through verse eleven and again mentioned that these verses were referred to as The Beatitudes and that they were spoken at The Sermon On The Mount.

The Prophet Ezekiel then asked everyone present to bow their heads in prayer, and he took off on his denouement: "O Gracious and Merciful Father, we all are resigned to the fact that we cannot possibly understand all of thy works, why some things happen while others don't, why some prayers are answered and others go unheeded, why some people prosper, and others, who try just as hard, fall by the wayside, and why one of our loveliest jewels, Teener Cline, has been plucked from our presence. Dear God we can only take solace in knowing that she is with You now and will remain so forever. Amen."

As the congregation raised their heads The Pophet looked over to organist Frances Hayes, nodding, and she broke into the old song of encouragement "Farther Along". "Please now stand and sing along with me the first and fouth verses. Gladys Cline tells me that it was Teener's favorite", he said smiling warmly at Mrs. Cline as her head bobbed up and down in agreement. "Number 235 in the Baptist Hymnal," The Prophet announced, and then began the song in his rich baritione.

"Templed and tried, we're oft made to wonder,
Why should it be thus all the day long;
While there are others living about us,
Never molested, though in the wrong."

The congregation sang along with The Prophet Ezekiel; then they followed his lead when he stepped up the volume on the refrain.

"Farther along we'll know more about it,
Farther along we'll understand why,
Cheer up, my brother, live in the sunshine,
We'll understand it all by and by".

Then as he began the fourth verse, as they had rehearsed, Blair Falls Houser and his associates came to the front and positioned the coffin enclosing the body of Teener Cline, turning it ninety degrees, and started to slowly roll it down the aisle toward the rear of the church. As one the Royal Ambassador Color Guard placed their hands over their hearts and followed lil' Teener's pink casket down the aisle.

"Often when death has taken our loved ones,
Leaving our home so lone and so drear,
Then do we wonder why others prosper,
Living so wicked year after year."

they sang , then as the entourage exited the sanctuary the rest of the mourners followed, beginning with the family and then the ensuing rows from front to back, all heading out to the graveside service. The Prophet Ezekiel stood watching from his place at the front of the church. He felt very,very, good with his performance, and he was well satisfied that this event would be a springboard for his evangelistic career. As he started down the aisle something caught his eye to his right and he stopped and turned to see Morris Hight standing in the side door, the door Blair Falls had carried him out earlier. Morris was holding a half empty pint of Bourbon De Luxe in his hand and tears were streaming down his cheeks. The Prophet Ezekiel walked over to Morris and hugged him, then plucked the bottle from his hand and killed it in three seconds, putting his arm around the besotted Morris Hight and escorting him to the graveside.

PART 4–REVIVAL

The Prophet Ezekiel pulled up in front of the Meadowbrook Supper Club down in the edge of South Carolina at 2:00 p.m., the appointed time he and Bill Ramseur had agreed upon. The Prophet walked into the familiar bar side, where all the booths and stools were; the left side of the building was totally open with tables and chairs set around. It was here that the former Zeke Taylor had spent many a Saturday drinkin' PBRs with his buddies. But that seemed a hundred years ago to The Prophet as he walked in the door and espied Bill Ramseur in a booth to the right; The Prophet's drinking days were purty much behind, although he would have a touch once in a while. He walked over and extended his hand to Bill Ramseur, who stood up from the booth grinning broadly. They sat down and Bill Ramseur nodded toward the longneck PBR sitting in front of The Prophet; "On me," he said, taking a long pull from the tall brown bottle in front of him. "So how have you been, The Prophet Ezekiel", asked Bill Ramseur, the hint of a smile at the corners of his mouth. The Prophet looked a little surprised at the way he had been addressed but recovered quickly and said "So I guess you are up to date on where I am in my journey?"The Prophet said, Bill nodding in agreement.

"I must say I think you thought things out right well, especially for a newcomer of your age. You are light years ahead of where I was in my early twenties; I was still whoring and drinking, and then got married to that slut from High Shoals. Course that didn't last so awful long, not after I found her in bed with Reverend Jake Rhyne that day I came home from work early. Anyway, the mental anguish and turmoil fomented my conversion to Christianity and the acceptance of our Lord Jesus Christ as my own very personal savior," Ramseur said.

"Amen, Brother Ramseur," The Prophet said, tipping up the PBR.

"As you aware, The Prophet Ezekiel, that was when I got involved with the Pentecostal Holiness Church, and after serving a brief apprenticeship at the Lucia Holiness Tabernacle up near Lincolnton, only a year, I struck out with my new wife, whom I met at the church, traveling North and South Carolina spreading the Gospel. We started out just pulling up in little towns and preachin' and singin' on the street corner. I could play chords on a guitar and Eileen would bang on her tambourine and I would preach and we would sing old Gospel songs. Then when I commenced preachin' Eileen would set the tambourine down in front of me and before you knew it quarters and fifty cent pieces and sometimes a little green would accumulate. We got to where we could stay in a room and have enough to eat on what we made, and then as time went on we were able to stay in an inexpensive motel some and put away some money. When I ran into a traveling evangelist down in Cheraw, South Carolina, who was fixin' to retire I reckon the stars were aligned and the price he wanted for his tent was reasonable; he even financed some of it and let me pay that part over a year. Yep, Eileen and I have been all over the southeast preachin' and singin' and testifyin'. Now I'll tell you, the Prophet Ezekiel, it has got a few patches on it, but it is not leakin' a drop right now, and we can go over there and turn the hose pipe on it to prove it. In fact, I insist on it. I have it set up on a field there on the Dallas-Stanley Highway right across from the Ramseur homeplace, where my mama still lives. Ya know she doesn't go along with my Pentecostal Holiness approach, being a life long Lutheran and all, but every year she has allowed me to come set up my tent for a week. It was kinda funny, 'cause she never came to a service, but she was good enough to let me set up there. And I have talked to her, and she is willing to let you do the same thing, set up there for a week a year at no cost."

The Prophet Ezekiel had been listening intently to Reverend Bill Ramseur; he trusted him, knowing the family and always having heard good things about him, even from people who weren't too crazy about Pentecostal Holiness Evangelists. The former Zeke Taylor had even played high school football against Reverend Bill Ramseur's younger brother, Mike.

Brian and Lucille, the owners, walked over to say hello to them. It was early, so they could still talk pretty well; The Prophet Ezekiel ordered two more more long neck PBRs for them.

"Well, Bill", The Prophet said, "I think your price you had mentioned when we talked on the phone of $800.00 is fair, considering it will hold a hundred people, but I wonder if you might think about maybe looking at things like the minister who sold it to you did".

"You mean financing a bit of it?" Reverend Ramseur asked, grinning at The Prophet.

"Exactly", said The Prophet, "and I will tell you that my wife Cinnamon and I have seven hundred dollars in our savings jar at home, so if you can give us a year to pay you the other hundred I'd say we have a deal". Reverend Bill Ramseur put on a big smile and took down half of the PBR that Brian had delivered; "I will agree to that, but I do want you to go over there to where the tent is set up across from my mama's house and let me turn the hose pipe on it. I would feel better about the transaction that way. Plus I have talked to mama, and she is willing to let you keep the tent on that site for a full six weeks, just to get you off to a good start; now mind you, after this six week period it will go back to just one week a year, understood?" Reverend Ramseur said, looking straight at The Prophet Ezekiel and not smiling. The Prophet understood the gravity of the situation and put out his hand, Reverend Ramseur quickly extending his, and the two evangelists had a deal.

The Prophet Ezekiel followed Reverend Ramseur to the Stanley Highway where his tent was set up. It was the standard light brown canvas type, essentially a greatly reduced version of a circus tent. Reverend Ramseur turned on the spigot and shot water all over the tent from one end to the other, repeating the process several times as The Prophet walked around inside looking for leaks. Satisfied that the tent was leak free, The Prophet drove the short distance to his trailer, secured the $700.00 that he and Cinnamon had saved, and hurried back to the tent, where Reverend Ramseur was waiting with two papers, one a bill of sale and the other a promissory note for $100.00 , due in full in one year's time, and just like that The Prophet Ezekiel had a tent. Reverend Ramseur told The Prophet that he would throw in the small generator which provided the limited lighting inside the tent as a gesture of good will, and made The Prophet promise him that he would let him know when the first service would be. With that The Prophet Ezekiel drove back home to tell Cinnamon that everything was set, they had a tent, and it was time to get the show on the road.

The next week The Prophet Ezekiel spent every evening over at the tent, rehearsing singing and preaching and securing folding chairs from various places. Blair Falls Houser even let The Prophet have fifteen chairs that were kind of tattered but still workable. They managed to pull together another thirty five chairs of different types to give them a total of fifty seats. When the two of them had gotten all of the chairs properly assembled in the tent The Prophet stood back and looked at the assemblage with an amused smile; it was quite a diverse assortment of seating, ranging from an old recliner to abandoned dining room chairs, and even one yellow plastic covered chrome legged kitchen table chair that Paul Ramseur's aunt, Wendell, had donated. The Prophet had set the time for the first preaching—-one week from the day he had purchased the tent. He felt like that would give them enough time to polish up the program. And just like when he was preaching under the sheets in his back yard people started coming and hanging around, more every night until Monday night, two days before the first service, The Prophet counted thirty people inside the tent. As he stood watching the group, a rather rotund figure in suspenders sporting two badges hanging on his belt, sheltered by his ample belly, caught The Prophet's eye. It was Inspector Huffmeister, the building inspector, come no doubt to relieve The Prophet of some cash.

"Good evening, The Prophet Ezekiel," Inspector Huffmeister said, grinning and exposing his snaggly teeth and squinting at The Prophet through his piggy red rimmed eyes. "Looks like the evangelistic world is smiling on you The Prophet Ezekiel. I hear you bought this tent and are gonna be here for six weeks. Is that right?" Huffmeister asked. "That is true, Inspector Huffmeister, and what can I do for you?" The Prophet Ezekiel said.

"Well, things have changed; this here tent is a lot different from those ragged sheets you had tied together over behind your trailer. What you got here is a much more permanent situation," the Inspector said, surveying the inside of the tent. "But it will only be here for six weeks," The Prophet offered. Inspector Huffmeister stuck his chubby thumbs inside his pants, right where his two building inspector badges hung and said "It's all relative my Prophet, it is all relative. Surely you will agree that a real canvas tent is certainly more of a permanent structure, and I am sure that you would also agree that having this tent out here with room for parking and everything sorta shoots this whole situation into more of a public structure. Why what in the world you gonna do if somebody wants to go to the bathroom?" The Prophet Ezekiel was dumbfounded; for once the inspector had said something that actually made sense. "Well I guess I kinda overlooked that," The Prophet said.

"Well, I understand that, you bein' new in the business and all, and I myself have been known to overlook things, you know what I mean, The Prophet Ezekiel?" The Prophet understood totally. "But Inspector Huffmeister,," The Prophet protested, "I just gave my last dime to Reverend Ramseur to buy this tent. I don't have a cent."

"I figgered that, The Prophet Ezekiel, so I am gonna do you a huge favor. I will give you three days of services to get a Porta Pottie here and bring me an envelope with five twenties in it." Huffmeister eyed The Prophet and grinned again; The Prophet Ezekiel, knowing he was had, nodded in agreement. "I would suggest one of them 'love offerings'," Inspector Huffmeister threw over his shoulder as he swaggered from the tent. The Prophet knew he had his work cut out for him, but he felt strong, and having gained confidence from his successful debut at Teener Cline's funeral, he was satisfied he would prevail.

The lanky man with the big brown teeth knocked on the door, and after hearing "Come in" walked inside the office of Dr. Charlie Glenn, Chief of the Psychiatry Department for the Western North Carolina Center for the Criminally Insane. "Please be seated", Dr. Glenn said, smiling benevolently and motioning toward a small wing backed chair that faced Dr. Glenn's large mahogany desk. Pasour Rhyne nodded solemnly and took his seat, then lifted his eyes to face the man who held his fate in his hands. Pasour Rhyne had been in the institution for eight years, and this was the second time Dr. Charlie Glenn had called him in. The word in the wards was there was never good news for you the first time Dr. Glenn talked to you, but the release rate was over fifty percent on the second trip.

Dr. Charlie Glenn continued to smile at Pasour Rhyne and began. "Mr. Rhyne, I understand that you have been here at our center for eight years now, is that correct?". "Yes, Dr. Glenn, eight years," Pasour replied. "And according to the documents I am looking at this very moment I see that you have spent your entire tenure here and have accrued no disciplinary infractions."

"I have no recollection of any", Pasour Rhyne said, looking blankly at the Doctor.

"And I also understand that you have undergone thirteen rounds of electro-shock therapy, and that you say that you feel fine presently and that you have absolutely no recollection of murdering a female evangelist by the name of Sister Alma in Dallas, North Carolina some eight years ago, correct?" When Dr. Glenn mentioned the name of Sister Alma Pasour Rhyne shuddered inwardly but was able to keep his totally calm outward composure.

"No, Dr. Glenn I don't remember that name and certainly do not recollect doing anything like that to anyone," Pasour said, changing his blank look to a more earnest one.

"Well, Mr. Rhyne, I have been in this field for over thirty years, and I have seen this sort of occurrence a couple of time, and mind you, it is rare. But electro-shock therapy works differently with each individual and according to the cases I have been around and involved with the total loss of memory of the incident is a very good sign of recovery, a very good sign," stated Dr. Charlie Glenn, picking his lit cigar up out of the ash tray on his desk and puffing on it vigorously. Pasour Rhyne noticed the little burn holes in the Doctor's starched white shirt. Shooting for his very best plaintive look Pasour asked, "Well, what does this mean, Dr. Glenn?"

"What it means , Mr. Rhyne, is that I have something for you," said Dr. Charlie Glenn, opening the drawer in front of his ample round belly and withdrawing an envelope with the address of the center in the upper left. Pasour noticed that it was addressed to him.

Pasour opened the envelope and read the following: "Dear Mr. Rhyne: After an extensive evaluation of your situation and your progress the Psychiatric Team of the Western Carolina Center for the Criminally Insane have concluded that the treatments you have received in your time here have cured you of any mental illness. I, Dr. Charlie Glenn, Chief of

THE PROPHET EZEKIEL

Psychiatry, concur with this conclusion and I hereby deem that you, Pasour Rhyne, are fit to return to society." It was signed by Dr. Charlie Glenn, and in the envelope was a one way ticket to Gastonia, North Carolina.

Pasour had sort of expected this to happen, and after the way Dr. Glenn was talking before he had handed him the envelope it was all he could do to contain himself; however, he had maintained his composure and his nonplussed demeanor while he read the letter, allowing himself to smile gently as he finished.

"Thank you Dr. Glenn, so much," Pasour Rhyne said, maintaining the benign smile. Dr. Charlie Glenn beamed at Pasour Rhyne and re-lighted his Havatampa Nugget cigar. Victories were few and far between at the Western Carolina Center, and Dr. Glenn was reveling in this one; he was satisfied that he and his team had brought a disturbed, pitiful human being back to a point where he could re-enter society and have some level of productivity. He stood up, holding his smile and extending his arm across the desk to shake hands with the murderer. Pasour Rhyne rose and walked to the front of the desk and shook hands with Dr. Charlie Glenn.

"Thank you Doctor, for all you have done for me," Pasour said, and let a little tear roll down his cheek. "Good luck to you Mr. Rhyne, and let us hear from you. You probably would prefer not to come back and visit," he chuckled as he clapped Pasour Rhyne on the shoulder.

"That would be true, Dr. Glenn, that would be very true," said Pasour Rhyne, his purplish lips skimming back to expose his large brown teeth. Pasour Rhyne then left the Doctor's office, and as he went out the door and got into the hall muttered to himself "No recollection of shooting her, what a friggin' joke; why, if she walked up to me again I would let her have it one more time—pow, right between the eyes." Pasour Rhyne giggled quietly as he walked back to his room to prepare for his trip home.

Pasour Rhyne's bus trip the next day to Gastonia was uneventful; Pasour had called his half-witted cousin Billy Ray and told him to meet him at the Trailways Station. Billy Ray was glad to pick him up; he did not work, had absolutely nothing to do, and welcomed any kind of deviation from his dull norm. Billy Ray got a government check every month, the product of a nasty motorcycle accident in which a portion of his frontal lobe was removed by a telephone pole.

"So ya okay now, Pasour?" Billy Ray asked as they drove down Highway 321 toward Dallas. They would take a left when they got to the Dallas Crossroads and head down the Cherryville Highway, then take another left onto White and Jenkins road when they got to the Costner Community. That was where Pasour Rhyne had gone to elementary school until he was in the fourth grade, when the Principal had met with his mother and explained that the school was just not equipped to deal with a boy of Pasour's age who still "soiled" his pants. Thereafter Pasour had remained at home, doing whatever. Pasour's nonagenarian mother still lived in the old two story clapboard siding house with the tin roof that Pasour had grown up in. She had been very excited to hear that her "boy" was coming home when Pasour had called her right after he hung up with Billy Ray, and she assured him that he would be very welcome both at home and re-entering into the community. Pasour knew his momma would want to see him, but he was not too certain how the rest of the people would feel. Pasour figgered he would just have to wait and see.

"Yep, Billy Ray, the head knocker psychiatrist up there says I am completely cured, so I guess I'll just have to take his word on it," Pasour said, as he grinned, pulling his purplish livery lips back over his brown teeth. "So what have I missed, anything exciting?" Pasour asked.

Billy Ray pondered a moment and brightened up as he remembered something. "Well, they's a new evangelist in town; he goes by the name of The Prophet Ezekiel and tonight is his first night in his new tent over there on the Stanley highway 'bout halfway 'tween Dallas and Stanley. I went over there one night last week and watched him and his wife practice——you know she helps him by singing and playing the tambourine and such," he said.

Pasour Rhyne had cringed inside when Billy Ray had said the word "evangelist" but he had hidden the reaction. Pasour had become a master of hiding his true feelings, as evidenced by his performance up at the Western Carolina Center for the Criminally Insane.

"Who is this 'The Prophet Ezekiel?'" Pasour asked. Billy Ray giggled and said "tain't nobody but ol' Zeke Taylor from up around Spencer

Mountain. He got religion when he was away at the Ranlo Prison Camp and decided he wuz gonna become an evangelist and got ol' Judge Bulwinkle to legally change his name to The Prophet Ezekiel." Billy Ray filled Pasour Rhyne in on the whole story, from The Prophet Ezekiel preaching under his sheet tent behind his single wide trailer to his buying Reverend Bill Ramseur's old tent. He even told Pasour about how Teener Cline had got run over in front of Bill's Food Center, and that her parents had gotten special permission from Reverend Fred Hight and Deacon William Hall to let "The Prophet Ezekiel" preach Teener's funeral. Billy Ray told all about the color guard there at Plainview Baptist Church and what a great talk The Prophet Ezekiel had given at the funeral.

"He even had a conversion right there at the graveside service just when they were getting' ready to lower Teener cline down into the ground; Morris Hight had been standing there beside The Prophet Ezekiel, kinda weepy but quiet like, when he started hollerin' 'help me, help me' at the top of his lungs. Well The Prophet Ezekiel sprung into action and grabbed ol' Morris around the shoulder with one arm and slapped his free hand up on Morris' forehead and looked him dead in the eye and said 'do you believe son, do you believe in Jesus Christ, your only savior, the Son of God who died for all our sins; do you accept Jesus Christ into your heart and soul and do you vow to follow him and his teachings from this day forward?' Ol' Morris Hight took to cryin' and sayin' 'oh yes, oh yes, The Prophet Ezekiel'. Pasour, I wuz standing right there across from them when it happened, and I can tell you I ain't never seen nothin' like it in my entire life. Why, when Morris said he accepted Jesus everybody there at the graveside commenced to clapping, even Blair Falls Houser's men, and I swear I saw a tear slide down ol' Blair's cheek. You oughta see them purty new teeth Blair has got; come all the way from Anderson, South Carolina.

Pasour Rhyne had been listening intently to Billy Ray's rambling monologue. "What does this woman look like," Pasour asked, getting an uneasy feeling inside even as he asked the question. "Why, hell, she's purty and wears tight shiny dresses and jumps around; she kinda reminds me of Sister Alma," Billy Ray said, immediately regretting bringing up the name of the late evangelist. But Billy Ray's regret increased ten fold as he watched his cousin's eyes get big and his jaws tighten.

"Why did you have to mention that sorry bitch's name," Pasour shouted as he grabbed Billy Ray by the shoulder, nearly causing the truck to run off the road. Pasour caught himself and released Billy Ray, apologizing profusely. "Billy Ray, I ain't got no idea what got into me; I am so sorry," he blubbered.

"Don't worry, Pasour, I'm alright", Billy Ray said, but he was still shaken by Pasour's outburst. Pasour was quiet for a few miles and then said "Billy Ray, how 'bout you come get me tonight and we ride over to see The Prophet Ezekiel's Revival." Billy Ray looked at his cousin, who was now smiling broadly.

"Well I guess I can; I'll be by at seven o'clock," Billy Ray said as they pulled up to the old clapboard house that had never been painted. Pasour Rhyne took his bag and got out of the truck and walked up to the L shaped side porch where his 94 year old mother waited to greet him, grinning her toothless grin. Billy Ray waved to both of them as he got back on to the road, wondering a little if Pasour Rhyne had really gotten "the cure".

It was opening night at "The Prophet Ezekiel Crusade" in the tent on the Dallas-Stanley Highway. The Prophet, after the visit form Inspector Huffmeister, felt a bit under the gun, but as he stood outside smoking a cigarette, a Lucky Strike straight drive, his fears started to vanish. The service was to commence at 7:30, and at 7:00 p. m. he counted twelve cars in the gravel lot, causing him to wonder if they would have enough chairs. "If there is a really big crowd that friggin' Huffmeister will probably show up and cause a problem," he thought to himself, but then dismissed that as paranoia, realizing that Huffmeister was all about money, and as long as The Prophet Ezekiel could come up with it he would be okay.

The Prophet Ezekiel felt good; the rehearsals had gone well, Cinnamon was getting into the swing of things shaking her tambourine and jiggling around in her plum colored sequined outfit with the slit on the side that went ten inches past her knee. The Prophet chuckled to himself as the thought struck him that his bride was about as sexy as the late Sister Alma had been. He thought a bit about his and Cinnamon's trip to see Polie Maxwell and how Polie had come to his end. But he mostly remembered Polie Maxwell's effusive goings on about his never ending love for Sister Alma. The Prophet could understand that kind of emotion; he realized that his feelings for his beautiful wife Cinnamon pretty much coincided with the way the late Polie had spoken of the late Alma. As The Prophet thought about these things he stepped around to the back of the tent and "while nobody was looking" pulled a thin flask from inside his suitcoat pocket, unscrewed the top and took three good drinks of Oodley Creek moonshine that Joe Keener had given him just this afternoon. Joe was a "rounder Bill", bootlegger and entrepreneur, and he had always liked the former Zeke Taylor. Joe, always a well spoken critter, had said "Good luck in your endeavor," and grinned at The Prophet as he handed him a quart mason jar of the best shine in Gaston County.

The Prophet stuck his flask back inside his coat and walked back to the front of the tent. He stationed himself at the entrance and greeted people as they came in. "Hello, Elmer, hello Bert," he said, smiling beatifically as he acknowledged the Chief Usher and organist for the late Sister Alma. "I swear, that is surely funny that those two would show up," The Prophet thought to himself. "I will take that as a good sign." As The Prophet greeted a few other people his ear was tuned to the music coming from the phonograph inside the tent; Cinnamon had selected "How Great Thou Art" by the famous George Beverly Shea. The Prophet loved that song, and it didn't hurt that Mr. Shea was associated with Dr. Billy Graham. Of course Dr. Graham was a very famous evangelist, and was a North Carolina boy.

"Yep, Cinnamon has come a long way in the last coupla weeks," The Prophet Ezekiel surmised as he stood there in front of the tent. She had become much more at ease in front of people, and he could tell that she was being well received. Her Sister Alma-esque burgeoning breasts were also a sizeable asset; her outfit tonight with a plunging neck line was sure to be an attention getter.

"Hello Billy Ray," The Prophet said as the slight, grinning little fellow walked by. The Prophet noticed a man with him that he did not recognize;

of course, there was not much to recognize, for he was wearing sunglasses, a Dallas High School Yellow Jackets baseball cap and a long coat. The man had his hands deep in the coat pockets. As the two walked by The Prophet Ezekiel burst into a broad smile as Blair Falls Houser came striding toward him. "Thank you for coming Mr. Houser, and thank you so much for those donated chairs," The Prophet said.

Blair Falls was not all dressed up like usual, but was wearing jeans and a flannel shirt, a smart black hat with a small red feather sitting atop his silver hair. "We were out riding horses earlier and cut it short so we could come out and see you," the genial undertaker said. Then, motioning toward the two people with him he said, "The Prophet Ezekiel, this is Sloan and Mae, two charter members of the Gaston County Horsemen's Association." The Prophet looked at the two: Sloan was a slender strong looking man with brawny forearms, and Mae was a busty redhead with slightly askew red hair, a good sized rear, and a very red face. The Prophet noticed a couple of pieces of straw clinging to Mae's riding breeches. The two smiled and went on in the tent with the President of the Horsemen's Association.

Pasour Rhyne and Billy Ray took a seat, Pasour on the yellow kitchen chair that Reverend Ramseur's aunt had donated and Billy Ray sprawled out in the tattered recliner. Billy Ray wanted to give himself a little distance from his cousin; Pasour had been acting a little strange ever since he had picked him up. First of all Pasour had snapped "None of you damn business" when Billy Ray had asked about his unusual attire. Then Pasour had been quiet for the whole ride, just sitting there silently behind those dark shades and fidgeting with something in his coat pocket. Billy Ray did not inquire any further.

Pasour Rhyne sat quietly on his yellow plastic chrome chair and listened to George Beverly Shea bellow out "How great Thou art, Then sings my soul , my savior God to thee, how Great Thou Art, How Great Thou Art. Pasour loved how ol' George would spread out the last four words of the song at the end. "Kinda funny, the last four words is the title of the song," Pasour thought to himself, giggling inside.

Then he reached inside his right coat pocket and fingered the snub-nosed thirty eight caliber pistol he had retrieved from the woodshed at his house. Of course it was not the gun that had been used to shoot sister Alma, that weapon being somewhere deep in the evidence room of the Gaston County Sheriff's Department, or in some Deputy's gun collection. This pistol was one he had cleaned and oiled heavily and wrapped up in a very oily rag the day before he murdered the evangelist. He remembered that he had chuckled to himself those years aago as he had hidden the pistol. "Ya always gotta have backup," he had said aloud, and cackled after he had said it. Pasour Rhyne had remembered exactly where he had hidden it, so he had no problem going straight to the gun; he had wiped it off real good and carried it way back into the woods and fired the .38. The gun had worked fine so Pasour was all set.

Ever since that Dumbass Billy Ray had said that the new evangelist's woman reminded him of Sister Alma Pasour Rhyne had been obsessing on two women: Sister Alma and whoever this Cinnamon woman was. Pasour remembered how Sister Alma had been so disrespectful of him, and the more he thought about it he began fantasizing about this Cinnamon girl, and everytime he would think of her her face would be fuzzy, just enough out of focus to keep one from seeing exactly what she looked like. But the Cinnamon body was not difficult; the Cinnamon body in Pasour Rhyne's mind was identical to Sister Alma's———the great breasts, the sequined dress with the slit halfway up the left leg. Pasour Rhyne had spent the rest of the afternoon pondering and fantasizing, trying to get the girl's face to come clear, but to no avail. He merely mumbled politely when his old mother would ask him a question. Finally the old lady gave up trying to talk to her son; she knew that sometimes he could get in some odd moods. So when he went back into his room and emerged in his outfit and announced that he was going somewhere with Billy Ray she didn't think much of it; she just stood in the doorway shaking her head slowly as the two of them departed.

The Prophet Ezekiel was standing on the little raised platform inside the tent looking out at the crowd; he swelled with pride as he noticed that every last seat was taken, even the old tattered recliner. As it was time for the show to begin he clapped his hands together to get everyone's attention. When they quietened he smiled and began.

"Ladies and gentlemen, let me welcome you to our gathering, on behalf of myself and my lovely wife Cinnamon." At this cue the luscious Cinnamon came from the rear of the little stage to stand beside The Prophet Ezekiel, grabbing his right hand with her left. "I, The Prophet Ezekiel, take great pride in the opportunity to be here tonight to serve you all in the name of Jesus Christ. It has been a long and arduous journey to get where we are; now please bow your heads: Dear Wondrous, omniscient, and all powerful God in heaven, we beseech you to bless this gathering of Christians, and we know that none of this would be possible were it not for your overflowing grace and forgiveness."

Pasour Rhyne looked around, his eyes shielded by his sunglasses; everyone had bowed their heads and closed their eyes, but his remained wide open, fixated on the face of Cinnamon. As The Prophet prayed Pasour Rhyne saw the haziness which had covered Cinnamon's face start to break up a little around the edges.

"And I want to testify in front of everyone here tonight how grateful I am to have been delivered from my evil ways, the drinking, the cursing, the sinning. And Lord, I want everyone to know I gave all of that up that wonderful night in prison when I accepted Your Son, Jesus Christ, as my personal Savior," The Prophet Ezekiel prayed.

Pasour Rhyne continued to stare at Cinnamon, and the face became clearer, the haze was disappearing until he could see her face totally——— the face of Sister Alma. Pasour Rhyne shuddered; he had a feeling that it would turn out this way. So as The Prophet Ezekiel droned on Pasour Rhyne pulled the pistol out of his pocket, stood up, and raised it toward cinnamon, who was only ten feet away. Then Pasour Rhyne's liver colored lips drew back, showing his giant brown teeth, and with a shout of "I knew it was you bitch" he pulled the trigger.

Cliff and Cleff Carpenter were standing outside Plainview Baptist Church. They were two of only a handful of people remaining at the church. The Dallas Funeral Home limousine had already departed, bearing the bereaved survivors, Blair Falls Houser himself behind the wheel.

THE PROPHET EZEKIEL

"Well what did ya think of that?" Cleff said. "It just beats anything I have ever seen."

"Yep Cliff, you are right about that." They were talking about how The Prophet Ezekiel had just concluded not only preaching his wife's funeral but also presiding over the graveside service.

"I halfway expected to see him jump in there with a shovel and start filling up the grave," Cliff chuckled, but caught himself and quickly said "no disrespect intended." The two diminutive men were twins and stood only 5'2" tall. They turned as one when they noticed that someone had come into their midst. Bothe of them smiled as they recognized Pastor Hight's son Morris. Morris was turning up a half pint bottle of bootleg Bourbon De Luxe and crying, tears running down his face. Apparently Morris had heard their conversation, for he blubbered "That ain't all The Prophet Ezekiel did, you just ain't heard the whole story."

"What you talkin' bout boy?" asked Cleff.

"Well I was right there when ol' Pasour Rhyne shot Cinnamon right between the eyes, so I saw The Prophet Ezekiel run to her side," said Morris. "He held her in his arms and felt for a pulse, but it was obvious she was gone. He then placed her body on the stage and looked at Pasour Rhyne, who was standing there screaming 'help me, help me'. He had dropped the pistol and was just standing there quivering. That was when The Prophet Ezekiel walked over to the man who had just killed his wife and put his arms around him and said 'Are you ready to accept Jesus Christ into your heart, to give up all of your evil ways, and to praise Almighty God from this day forward?'"

'Yes, The Prophet Ezekiel, oh yes, yes, yes,' Pasour Rhyne cried, and that's how The Prophet Ezekiel saved the man who had just shot his wife. And that's why you saw that man in shackles at the service; The Prophet Ezekiel had made a special request that Pasour Rhyne be allowed to attend."

The twins looked at each other as Morris Hight meandered away, draining the bottle and opening a fresh one from his hip pocket.

"Damned if that don't take the cake," Cleff said as the two men walked to their cars. "Bout the wildest thing that's happened around here since that Methodist preacher turned himself into a woman by getting' that operation."

"You are right about that," said Cliff, "but you know there was one good thing about that sex change thing."

"And what was that," Cleff bit, knowing a little about his twin's sense of humor.

"Well since his name was Ronnie he didn't have to change his name——ya know that name will work for either sex," Cliff said, chuckling.

"Truly a blessing, brother," said Cleff, " truly a blessing."